SOLITAIRE FOR 2

SOLITAIRE FOR 2

by Neil Mullarkey

Based on the feature film
by Gary Sinyor

B🍃XTREE

First published in Great Britain in 1995 by Boxtree Ltd,
Broadwall House, Broadwall, London SE1 9PL.

Copyright © 1995 Cavalier Features Limited
Copyright (text) © 1995 Neil Mullarkey

10 9 8 7 6 5 4 3 2 1

ISBN: 0 7522 0886 1

A CIP catalogue entry for this book is available from
the British Library

Cover design by Martin Lovelock

Typeset in Sabon by SX Composing Ltd, Rayleigh, Essex
Printed and bound in Great Britain by Cox and Wyman Ltd,
Reading, Berkshire

Acknowledgments

I'd like to thank the following: first and foremost, Gary Sinyor, both for his screenplay and for (along with his co-producer, Richard Holmes) asking me to write this novel; Clare Hulton, my editor, for agreeing with them, and being so helpful and encouraging; everyone involved in making the film – the actors, notably Jason Isaacs and Roshan Seth for their extra help, and the crew, but especially Nikki Zimbler and Michael McAloon in the production office, and the editor Ewa J. Lind and her assistant Cornelia Brown for furnishing me with early versions of the film; Nick Donovan for supplying me with details of the Survival Game.

I would also like to thank Dallas Smith and Irina Brook.

Laura Ashley supplied the interiors of Daniel's, Katie's and Harry and Caroline's homes in the film *Solitaire for 2*, as well as Katie's wardrobe.

To Joe and Kathleen

Chapter One

'Bifffff! A hard right and he was down. In a heap. She'd taken him totally by surprise.

She? He looked up as she strode down the corridor, not looking back to admire her handiwork. Not since playing rugby at school and having to go and see the nurse had he been so severely winded. And now he'd been felled by a kick from a woman (about the same age as that nurse) and for what? He'd been bending down to tie his shoelace. He'd been aware of people coming out of a nearby door, including a woman. He'd seen her feet come by, and stop by him, but he'd never thought he was in for a one-sided boxing match. He'd never met the owner of the punch, hadn't said anything to her. He'd looked up at her, yes – but who wouldn't? He'd been intrigued by her ankles.

She wore flat, sensible shoes and white tights under a long cream skirt that didn't give much above the knee away, even with some of the buttons undone, but merely hinted at the slim female form inside. As he slowly looked up, he'd taken in her jacket; smart, but not overly formal, like a man's jacket, a slightly darker cream than the skirt. Then he looked up at her face. She had beautiful eyes that had peered down at him with interest. Lips that he thought would make the purveyors of collagen green with envy. Mid-length, walnut-coloured hair.

She'd been looking down at him. Why shouldn't he look back? And smile even? She'd smiled, raised her eyebrows, he'd thought, in what could have been taken for lasciviousness. He'd increased his smile, and let his eyes wander downwards. Then – Biff! What was it all about? Why had she punched him? And so hard? If someone was going to punch him, he would have expected some aggressive behaviour at least, some predatory posturing, or at least the simple question – 'You staring at me or chewing a brick?' with the questioner happily providing their own answer.

Daniel Becker struggled to his feet, and continued along his way to give another lecture in his series on control in the social interface. *How to Lose Friends and Influence People* was the title of his book, which had won him a certain notoriety on review pages and Radio Four discussion programmes. He'd clashed with Dr Murray Henry, the popular breakfast TV psychologist, who had hammered his book in the *Guardian* and gone on to call him a 'twerp' on Radio Four's *Monday Morning*. Daniel had responded by calling into question the academic rigour of a man who appeared twice weekly on breakfast television wearing V-neck pullovers, sporting the sort of hair colour available only in the more exclusive salons of Kensington, and who did commercials for Trim Tummy low-fat meals.

As Daniel passed the glossy piece of cardboard depicting his thirty-year-old face, the sleeve of his book and various assorted images of modern life which greeted those who entered his seminars, he dusted himself down, and adjusted his tie. He wanted to look sharp, not like someone who'd just been punched to the ground by a girl. He checked his white shirt, his waistcoat (it belonged to his girlfriend and was designed by Hiro Hamachi, who had made his name by designing the puce mohair boiler suit, cut to the thigh, worn by last year's Best Actress winner on Oscar night) and dark, classically smart, blazer. Luckily, Harry hadn't seen the incident. Harry was his best friend, a little older, and, Harry liked to think, a little wiser than Daniel. Harry would have giggled and said, 'I think she fancies you.'

2

Harry enjoyed the verb 'to fancy'; as an American its English cosiness amused him. Daniel was used to girls fancying him, not walloping him in the stomach. His dark good looks, his deep brown eyes, his confident charm, coupled with his sometimes boyish immaturity endeared him to many, and only those who'd known him a very long time were inclined to feel like hitting him.

It had been a full morning already. He'd done the moody - looking - out - the - window - while - listening - to - Mozart's - *Requiem*-while-she-makes-coffee bit for Lucy, his girlfriend, now his ex-girlfriend. He would miss Lucy, but after six months he wasn't sure where it was going; whatever that meant.

'Maybe we should slow things down a bit,' she'd said, as he stared out of the window, not even taking his coffee. His non-committal shrug had sent her scurrying. It had worked out just the way Daniel liked. Neatly. No big scene, no tears and breakdowns, just a sullen packing of the overnight bag and she was off, and he could drop the blue toothbrush (which he'd provided for her on their first night together) in the bin. He'd done the decent thing, or given an impression of doing it, by running after her car down the street, barefoot and in his dressing-gown, the one he bought at the Hyde Park Hotel, because he'd liked it and its fluffiness, even though it had been far too expensive.

As soon as he was back in his flat, though, Mozart came off, and gave way to 'Love is the Drug' by Roxy Music. Daniel loved its insistent beat. He breathed a sigh of relief. A decision had been made. Now he could start flirting again, without feeling guilty. With the sheets changed and the toothbrush dispatched he could face the day, and twenty minutes later he emerged in the street once again, dressed and ready for life. He got into his car. It was flashy, which Daniel knew and enjoyed. It was turquoise, registration K19 MGR, apposite for an MG convertible, though in his more idle moments he wondered what else the letters could stand for – 'Macho Guy Rocks', 'Mmmm, Girls – React!', 'My Gosh – Raunchy' – but had dismissed these as stupid or syntactically flawed, and pondered how he could change his name to make it fit the letters . . . Michael Gus Roche, Mark Graham Rollins, Manuel Guido Rawlinson . . . but he'd decided not to waste any more time on that game. He had once looked into buying a registration plate with DB1, but when he found out that it cost about the same as a studio flat in Lincolnshire, he'd decided against it. He hadn't bought the flat in Lincolnshire either.

He headed off to work. It was a bright, but not particularly sunny day. Nevertheless, he drove with the top off and sunglasses on because he felt sunny. He smiled as he zipped through the streets of Maida Vale and Little Venice, tapping the steering wheel in time with the music from his in-car CD, Bryan Ferry still enquiring if you couldn't see that love was the drug for him.

He rounded a corner and pulled up outside a newsagent. Every day he went through this routine, picking up his *Independent* and various magazines, but today a traffic cop, passing on her motorbike, took exception to his parking on a double yellow line. He emerged to find her writing out a ticket, unswayed by the music blaring from his car. Daniel took in the scene in an instant, looked around, spotted a Mothercare store nearby, and rushed into it.

Who could punish a proud new father? Not this policewoman, and she cheerily tore up the ticket as she surveyed the two large boxes of nappies and helium balloon announcing IT'S A BOY! with which Daniel appeared. He shook her hand, and he took her by surprise with a little kiss on the cheek. He sped off, the balloon hanging on grimly by the flimsiest piece of string.

Two mothers with pushchairs and babies were some-what alarmed by the car that screeched up to them, and even more so by the excited young man in sunglasses who leapt out at them offering armfuls of nappies and a balloon. In his excitement Daniel let go of the balloon, and it escaped. The bemused mothers gratefully accepted the gift, keeping a wary eye out for Jeremy Beadle, as the balloon floated off to a new but probably short life floating over London.

As Daniel drove along the Westway and through central London he thought about Lucy, babies, relationships, book sales, nappies, the title of his next book, Lucy, Harry and what advance he could get, whether kissing the police-woman had been too much, babies, Harry's wife Caroline (an old friend from university to whom he had introduced Harry), petrol fumes, commitment, Hampstead Heath, toothbrushes, a possible trip to the States, paint-gun shoot-ing, Caroline and Harry's daughter Clare, the balloon, making love with Lucy, whether he'd have to rewrite the American edition of his book (they would have to change words like 'marvellous' to 'marvelous', and 'defence' to 'defense', and they'd emphasise the first syllable when reading it out, 'dee-fence') and lots of other things too trivial even to be conscious of.

At a red light, even though he was way back in the traf-fic, he stood up in his car, honked his horn and waved animatedly to the girl unsuccessfully offering windscreen-washing to the cars ahead of him. She had a delightful smile, long blonde hair and a carefree air that Daniel found very appealing. She duly cleaned his windscreen, and, much to the annoyance of the drivers behind, who honked at him, Daniel waited, pointing out little specks of dirt on the windscreen until satisfied that the very last one had been removed.

He arrived at the Self Centre, where he worked. It was in a grand building, erected in Victorian times before notions such as cashflow projections, heat retention, modems, lagging, or the information superhighway ever existed. It stood as a monument to a time when Britain still considered itself great in things other than simply ice-skating, small-bore shooting and Academy Awards. It had probably been built as the headquarters of a public utility (long since relocated to somewhere up the M40, to a large block with smoked glass windows, air-conditioning, lower ceilings made out of square polysomething tiles, and open-plan offices with electric sockets in the middle of the carpet tiles), but had now been converted to a multi-functional office amenity centre for a number of small businesses.

Daniel reversed into a space between two parked cars – not easy, as it was a tight squeeze – and congratulated himself with a smile once he'd achieved it, only to find the fit too tight for him to be able to open the car door, so he had to lever himself out.

He found the foyer and stairs full of humanity; well, humanity and pipes, glasses, tweed and beards. 'Who are they, Harry? What are they?' Daniel demanded upon seeing his friend also trying to fight his way through.

'Scientists.' Say no more, thought Daniel, and began to stagger a bit. Harry looked at him, and asked rather too loudly, 'Are you feeling okay?'

'I feel a bit . . .' Daniel didn't finish, so Harry picked him up with a confident fireman's lift that made Daniel let out an involuntary groan. Harry carried him up the stairs and through the sea of scientists with lots of explanatory mutterings like, ''Scuse me,' and 'Man down,' along the way through the now parting sea of pipe/tweed/beard until they reached a clear landing. This was clearly a well-rehearsed routine, and Daniel quickly recovered. They had to do this quite regularly. The Self Centre was always busy. There were plenty of customers for its particular brand of self-improvement, which didn't come cheap. On offer were many courses including art therapy, stress management intensive relaxation, and 'The Telephone – Your Friend Not Your Enemy', as well as Daniel's 'Personal Power' seminars.

Daniel nodded as Harry departed with a cheery, 'See you later.' He looked down at his shoes. They'd been his treat to himself when he'd heard the book had gone into its second reprint. They weren't that expensive, just black and built to last. It was then that he noticed his lace needed tying, bent down, and noticed a pair of female ankles wander into view . . .

Daniel kept replaying the punching scene in his mind as he conducted the seminar that morning. Maybe he was harder on them than he would normally have been. After an hour or so it was time for the first role-play game, and he knew exactly who he would choose. The one in glasses who'd arrived late. He loosely set up the situation. A man sits writing at a large desk. He's busy. This part was to be played by Bob Narley, an actor who often helped Daniel out. He was tall, with aquiline features, and vaguely reminded one of the lead singer of Spandau Ballet. He was in shirt sleeves and acting busy. Very Busy.

A knock at the door. In the exercise the man in glasses had to bring in some figures. 'Yes,' said Narley, still Terribly Busy, and in came the man in glasses, a bundle of nerves in blue trousers, brown comfortable shoes, blue pinstripe jacket, purple and dark blue tie.

7

'I've, umm, brought those figures you wanted.'

'Right,' said the other, too busy to look up from his work. The nervous man retreated, blinked and pushed his glasses up his nose, even though they hadn't slipped down. As he retreated he bumped into Daniel.

This role-play game, complete with a little office 'set', was being watched by a group of besuited men in *Mastermind* leather armchairs in the seminar room; a large, high-ceilinged room that had probably been built as a showpiece boardroom, but was now sensibly carpeted in user-friendly blue. The businessmen came from all sorts of backgrounds. Some were there at their own expense, some had been sent by their companies – small, medium, and large companies anxious to do anything in order to Maximise Performance in Middle, Upper-Middle, and Senior Management.

Daniel looked at the hapless man who'd brought in the figures. 'Okay, Mr Parris. What's going through your mind?' Nothing, apparently. But really there was. A great deal, though not all of it conscious . . .

'Can I go home, now? I don't want to be on this course any more; I didn't really want to give him those figures; What figures, anyway? Why can't he pick on somebody else? When's lunch? Should I eat the cheese and pickle, or the tuna and sweetcorn sandwich first? Did Julie pack me any crisps? I hope they're ready salted, because salt 'n' vinegar make my lips all itchy; I worked out that this is costing about twenty quid a minute, or was it per second? I wish Julie hadn't made me come on the course.'

But Julie had. She reckoned he needed to be more pushy. She'd read about chutzpah, and although she couldn't pronounce it, she thought it sounded like something her husband could do with. After all, he wasn't getting any younger, and should be getting on better at work. Mr Sharples had passed him over for promotion. Twice. Parris had told her the other candidates were very good, but Julie had told him he was good too, and he'd reluctantly had to agree.

He'd arrived a bit late for the first seminar. He'd helped a woman with a pushchair and baby up the escalator on the Underground, and the baby had kicked him in the groin while he was helping carry it and its pushchair up the stairs. It meant that he'd come out of the wrong exit, so he'd had to find his way back to the right exit, but you couldn't go back in the way he had come out. So he'd had to go all the way round at street level, but there was a big roundabout and nowhere to cross, and lots of railings that he didn't want to jump over. By then he was getting late, so he'd had to run, and had got a bit sweaty. When he'd got to the seminar room, all the suits were sitting in their *Mastermind* chairs and Daniel Becker was making them look at the ceiling because that's where the limit of their ambition should be.

Parris had asked if this was the self-assertiveness course (he'd missed the glossy cardboard thing outside), and Daniel had sent him out telling him to come in and ask again. Four times he'd done this. Daniel had hoped he'd come back more confident, but each time he came back more diffident. By the fourth time Parris had decided that if nobody answered this time he'd go and eat his sandwiches in the park and go home in time for *Neighbours* and *Going for Gold*. But Daniel did answer the fourth time.

'Is this the self-assertiveness course?' asked the weary Parris.

'No.'

'Oh.'

'This is the course on control. And you must be Mr Parris.'

'Yes, I'm sorry I'm late. There was this pushchair, you see . . .'

9

'Don't be sorry.'

'No, all right.'

'Will it happen again?'

'Umm . . . No.'

'No.'

'No.'

'No.'

'Take a seat.'

'Err . . . right . . . umm . . .'

'The one in which nobody is sitting.'

'Yes, right, sorry.'

'Don't be sorry.'

'No, all right.'

Daniel sighed. He could only guess what had been going through Parris's mind as he brought in the figures. He himself was still thinking about that female punch; pain had turned to anger. 'What's going through Mr Parris's mind? Anyone?' Hands went up, and one grey suit with glasses volunteered a hand. This was Norman Waddle, a pleasant man with a solid but, as yet, unspectacular career (but perhaps that would change after this course?) with the finance house Gilzean Delaney Shreeves Hart. 'He's afraid,' offered Waddle.

'How do we know he's afraid?' Daniel asked. No more hands went up, so he answered himself. 'We look for the signs. Notice he doesn't look his boss in the eye. What about his body language?' Parris wasn't sure whether to look at him or not, and blinked a bit. This was all bread and butter to Daniel. He'd stressed this point time and time again. Not that it wasn't lucrative – it certainly was that – but he could see this was a rather slow group. 'He's frightened to turn his back,' suggested another businessman, someone in oil who'd been to Cambridge with that bloke off the telly who presented that panel game with funny

10

objects and old footage on BBC2, and did the voice for Billy Burger in Burger Hut commercials.

'OK. What else?' No response. Good. He could move effortlessly into one of his favourite segments of the presentation, with several of his favourite buzzwords – attitude, body language, power, confidence, authority. These were all good words. Daniel enjoyed them.

'What we are dealing with here is attitude,' explained Daniel, as he strode over to the side of the room. He moved a mauve silk cloth to reveal a gun. Parris gulped. Would he have to pay the ultimate sacrifice for his flawed body language? Daniel picked up six bullets, and loaded the gun as he continued back to Parris.

'Change the attitude of a person, you change his body language. Give a person power, let them *assume* power –' to Parris's increasing anxiety, Daniel casually pointed the gun at the wall behind the businessmen and fired. Bang! The incredulous businessmen all swivelled and looked at the wall, spattered with bullet holes, ' – even if they don't actually have it, and that person will act with confidence and authority.' The gun was a great prop, and Daniel clearly enjoyed it.

Parris stared at him with fear and bewilderment – and admiration, even. This man had chutzpah with a capital 'ch'. Parris had only fired a gun at the fair before, the sort you shoot at ducks to win a goldfish or bottle of Pomagne or Scrappy-Doo alarm clock. It had given him a nosebleed. Luckily, he'd been able to stem the flow of blood with the cuddly pink vole that Julie had won at one of those pick-things-up-in-the-glass-box-with-the-mechanical-hand machines; she'd actually been going for the Casio digital watch, and had spent £12.90 in ten pees on it.

Daniel slipped the gun into Parris's pocket, and told him to do it again. Parris took a deep breath, and went round the side of the set and knocked. Loudly. Confidently. 'Yes,' said the Busy Man, anxious to get back to his crossword; Bob Narley didn't really feel he should be doing this sort of thing, but it paid better than children's theatre, and he managed to get the crossword done most days before coffee and biscuits.

Parris slipped into the room. Chutzpah Incarnate, his hand checking his gun. He strode to the desk.

'What is it?' said Narley, slightly unnerved by the look in Parris's eye; he did this role-play every week, sometimes twice if there was an evening group, but he'd never seen quite such a look.

'I brought you those figures you wanted.' The servant who brought the head of John the Baptist to Salome could not have been more confident than Parris with his figures, which he placed on the desk before turning and walking towards the door. Lights up, and applause, which Parris modestly accepted while giving the gun gingerly back to Daniel before returning to his seat, trying to keep his head down.

Daniel was about to launch into his next monologue when he saw Harry sidle in. Taking in Harry, he began, 'Power . . . is control. Remember that. Control is the key to the door of success. If you don't believe you're nervous, you won't be. If you don't believe you can win that deal, you won't win it. The trick is to give yourself your own imaginary gun.'

Norman Waddle interjected, 'When you say trick, you make it sound like it's just a game.'

Daniel reacted with fury. 'Not *just* a game! There's no such thing as "just" a game. Life is a game. With set rules. And winners. And losers.' A dismissive nod of his head emphasised his point; Daniel was pleased with himself. This was a good point for coffee and biscuits. He headed towards the door, but was stopped in his tracks by another question from Something in Oil.

'Does that apply to women?'

Daniel turned, and said gravely, 'Most of all.'

Harry was rather concerned about his friend. He'd not seen such unprovoked anger for a long time. As Daniel strode down the corridor ahead of him, he shouted to him 'Hey, hey, you all right?'

'Fine,' replied Daniel, a big smile coming over his face. 'Did you like the outburst? I've been working on expression of anger. That was sort of ... explosion, but my suppressed is pretty good, too.'

Harry was taken aback. 'Oh no, you – '

Daniel was pleased. 'You believed it. Now that's a compliment, Harry.'

Harry smirked. 'Well, you've got them eating out of the palm of your hand.'

'How about you?'

Harry grunted, 'Aeah.' Daniel wanted to know what the grunt meant.

'Which "aeah" is that? The "I'm not sure" aeah? Or the dreaded "I am sure but I'd better keep quiet" aeah?'

'Actually, it's my "I hear you got floored by a woman" aeah.'

'Aeah,' replied Daniel. He'd hoped nobody knew, least of all Harry. This could mean a week or two of ribbing. And he didn't want that. Especially when he had rather fancied his assailant, and had hoped to meet her again, in rather more felicitous circumstances. 'You look tense,' said Harry. 'How about some relaxation. On me.'

Daniel sat in shadow, painting at an easel. Harry sat in an armchair watching his friend.

'I still can't believe people pay for this.'

13

Harry tried to quieten him by speaking in hushed tones. 'Sssh. Keep painting.'

Daniel was not an ideal subject for art therapy.

Harry's work mainly involved helping businesspeople reduce stress. They used one side of their brain too much in their work, leaving the other side – the creative side – undernourished. To restore equilibrium, Harry put them in a darkened room with soft lighting and sea and whale noise to create the impression of being deep underwater, far away from stress, from the *Financial Times*, from Canary Wharf, from faxes and in-house memoranda.

'Therapeutic nonsense,' spat Daniel.

Harry gave him a look that said, 'Shut the fuck up and paint,' but which he hoped said only the second bit. Daniel was still riled about the punching in the midriff incident, and the fact that Harry knew.

'So you heard about this morning?'

'Sssh . . . who was she?'

Daniel had no idea. He'd had no warning, no apology. Nothing. 'I must have days like this more often. One girl clocks me, another leaves me, and it's only midday.'

Harry's amazement at this news meant he forgot himself and his hushed tones. 'Lucy left you?'

'Sssh,' admonished Daniel.

Harry went back to whispering, with a touch of frustration. He couldn't understand: yesterday Daniel had said it was serious. But that was yesterday; that was Daniel. He claimed she'd started an argument about nothing, and left. Harry knew this was bullshit, and said so.

'No look! OK, OK, it's bullshit,' said Daniel.

Daniel put down his brush. He looked at his friend for advice. Another relationship had failed and perhaps Harry could help him understand why.

'Is it me? I mean why can't I hold down a relationship?

14

Can you see any sort of a pattern – is there something I'm doing wrong?'

Harry was non-committal. He said he didn't know, but Daniel sensed he thought he did. It was in his eyes, said Daniel, even though he could barely see them in the dim marine lighting. 'If you want someone to believe you, you've got to look them in the eyes.'

Harry looked Daniel in the eyes. He still wouldn't be drawn.

'I don't know. Better?' said Harry.

'You're lying, Harry. Your arms say it all. Almost begging me to believe you.'

Harry's arms were indeed raised as if in supplication. Daniel was not averse to lecturing even his closest friends on body language techniques. Daniel really wanted Harry's help.

'Come on, you can tell me. What are friends for?'

In the years that Harry had known Daniel, he'd seen a succession of girls come and go through Daniel's affections.

There was that girl with the exquisite voice, who did traffic reports from a helicopter for different radio stations in different guises. She was the Eye in the Sky for City FM, Airborne Alison for Metro-Talk, and Zelly Q for Rhythm FM. In reality she was Sally Pangbourne, who'd never quite sorted out what she wanted to do since leaving St Andrew's University with a modest degree in French and Norwegian. She'd had a bit of a reputation up there, not helped by being found in a gorse bush on the famous golf course (the Old Course, for which there was a six-month waiting list to even play, and where jeans were not allowed) by an aged steward on an aged moped, with the captain of the rugby Second XV. At least neither was wearing jeans, but they weren't wearing much at all.

15

She'd met Daniel at a cinema, in a matinée audience of five, waiting to see an Italian Best Foreign Film Oscar winner. They found themselves the only ones laughing at the trailer for the French film, which that year had had the temerity to gross as much in France as the latest Hollywood blockbuster, but had generally been dismissed by the British critics as typically French humour and therefore not funny. Then they began giggling at the same bits in the Italian film, unsure whether they were laughing because they thought it was genuinely funny, or because the other was and this was a safe form of flirting. When the lights came up at the end they checked each other out, then went and had cocktails at the Café de Paris. And six months later Daniel was playing Mozart's *Requiem* and throwing away her toothbrush.

There was that girl on the marketing conference in Guernsey. It was a bit of a junket in the name of management training. Daniel did the afternoon, and Smokie did the evening, including their hit, 'Living Next Door to Alice'. Unlike them, he hadn't waited twenty-four years to ask for a chance, and had rather drunkenly got off with this woman who marketed NutraSweet. When telling Harry, Daniel couldn't remember her first name, but did remember her surname was Hicks because the pin in her name-tag had stuck in his shoulder in a particularly passionate moment. Ms Hicks had taken the pin off as well as the jacket, but somehow they'd never quite recaptured the fire of that pre-'ouch' moment.

Then there was Lucy, who was in PR. Her clients included the Banana Council, which meant she often had to go out on the road with Bananaman, and would frequently try out new products on Daniel, like banana curry, banana cheese and banana crisps. She also represented the British Sofa Council, and those snacks in foil bags like croûtons with chives, potato-skin-and-sour-cream nibbles, or those with names where you pronounced the consonants differently from usual – jalapeño, tortilla.

Harry took a breath and shared his opinion with his friend. 'Right. OK. They don't fail. You self-destruct them.'

Daniel was a little taken aback. Self-destruct? Why would he want to do that? That's what tapes did in *Mission Impossible* in five seconds.

'And don't even try to deny it,' continued Harry, gathering momentum. 'You don't want to hold down a relationship.'

Daniel bridled. 'Maybe I just haven't found someone I want to hold down a relationship with.'

Harry let some anger creep into his hushed tones, 'Maybe . . . You manipulate every woman you go out with, so that she falls in love with you, so that you can claim it's unbalanced so that you can manipulate them into leaving you.'

Somehow the truth was harder to take in the dark. Daniel switched on the little Anglepoise light above his painting. It was a mess of black paint and he felt defensive, 'So that's what friends are for. To kick a man when he's down.'

'I've hardly tapped you on the shoulder.' Harry got up and looked at Daniel's effort. 'It's a bit like a child cast adrift on an endless ocean.'

Daniel pulled it off the easel, and walked out. Harry got up to follow. He wondered if he had been too hard. No, Daniel had pleaded for the truth, and that's what he'd given him. Besides, he'd liked Lucy.

Chapter Two

A group of eight-year-olds were playing, boys and girls together in the garden. One of the boys had a water pistol, and was chasing the others, all squealing as they tried to avoid getting hit. They ran round the side of the house. One little girl in a gingham dress was sitting in a sandpit, oblivious to the fun going on behind. She took the attention of the water pistol-wielding boy, so he let the others go. He crept up on her, and got up right behind her, the weapon poised behind his back. He turned to check that the others were watching: yes, they were. Suddenly the sandpit girl stood up, hit the boy square on the jaw, knocking him over, and sat down again as though nothing had happened.

Twenty years later, an assembled group of scientists were listening intently to a lecture. They were a sea of tweed, beards, pipes and boredom, despite the fact that the lecturer was a beautiful woman. She had lost their interest with her fast, very dry delivery: no gimmicks, no emphatic language – she let the facts speak for themselves.

'In conclusion, my findings prove that the remains found by my colleague Dr Sandip Tamar are indeed those of a *homo habilis* and not a *homo sapiens*.'

In a way, she was still playing around in sandpits, only now it was her job, and it was called palaeontology.

One of the scientists, Lloyd Park, had come all the way from Cardiff for this and was none too impressed. He'd let his attention wander. Next to him sat Bill Something-or-other – Lloyd couldn't remember, but he had recognised him from that anthropological conference in Cambridge last summer when they'd both got pissed in the student bar. They'd renewed their acquaintance at coffee and biscuits. Bill managed to stifle a yawn.

'For ease of reference, we have named this fossil S 1762 G4.'

Was that it? Lloyd was disappointed. Couldn't they have come up with something better than that? What about Punjab Man? He wondered what he would call any remains he found. Trevor (after his best friend)? Iuean (after his dad)? Fatty (if it was fat)? Thinny (if it was thin)? Cardiff Man? He wondered if he could make up a name for it. Gralaglo? Varclet? Breeeeeeeefffufufaaaaaaaaaaaah? It struck him he might have had too much coffee at coffee and biscuits. Or what about a vaguely rude-sounding name? Clunge? Miff? Porco? Dimph? Nobody could touch him for it – if they found it rude, that was their problem, not his.

Bill leaned over. 'No 3D graphics. No simulations. No working models.' They both shook their heads in disapproval. Suddenly, Bill let out a yawn.

'Dr Tamar is continuing his work in India and we believe that more important discoveries will be made in the foreseeable future.' She looked up. Despite a general effort at stifling, the yawning was audible, and she could see how bored they all were.

'Thank you,' she said, a little taken aback by the wave of apathy.

Daniel and Harry were walking along a corridor. Daniel was staring disconsolately at the ground. Harry teased him, 'Hunched shoulders? Dragging feet? Is this a sulk by any chance?'

'No.'

It was, clearly. 'It is a sulk. Good. Would you like me to kiss it better?'

Suddenly the scientists emerged from the lecture hall, with Lloyd and Bill in the vanguard. In the hurry food-wards they almost knocked Harry over, making him spill his papers on the floor. The scientists headed off down the corridor, intent on lunch, at least two of them hopeful of a little post-prandial beer and darts.

Harry gathered his papers, stood up, and saw his friend intently looking through the small round window in the lecture hall door.

'Harry, Harry . . . It's her!' exclaimed Daniel.

Harry took a peek with him. She was clearing up her notes. Now Harry understood why Daniel had been in such a sulk. He obviously fancied her, and had probably tried some line on her that had gone wrong, but had then pretended it was totally unprovoked. She was striking, her beautiful eyes now scanning her pages of notes before putting them away in her bag.

'Look at the way she's handling her notes. Like love letters,' whispered Daniel.

She finished putting her notes away, and closed her briefcase.

Daniel was getting rather worked up, saying out loud to himself, 'OK, she's coming. Think of something. Think of something.' Harry couldn't believe it. He was going to try and talk to her?

'But she's already hit you.'

Daniel was ebullient. 'She hit me because she likes me. It's standard courtship.' Not that standard, thought Harry. 'Pre-pre-foreplay,' added Daniel, his confidence growing.

'Pre-pre-?' Harry was bewildered by his friend.

Daniel's pep-talk to himself continued, 'Come on,

20

Danny, think.' Suddenly an idea struck, 'Of course. Copy behaviour,' and he grabbed Harry's notes. According to Daniel, the theory of copy behaviour went something like this: do exactly the same as the other person, and this agreement of the body will soon lead to agreement of the mind. It was something he explained every week in his seminars, and had fun demonstrating with sketches and videos of chat shows.

Dr Katie Burrill picked up her briefcase. She knew they'd been bored, but that was their problem, not hers. She was at the cutting edge of anthropological research and if they weren't fascinated by the breakthroughs she and Sandip were making, then she wasn't going to jazz it up just for them. They'd made an exciting discovery, and that's all there was to it. In years to come S 1762 G4 would be talked about as a watershed. She put on her cream raincoat.

All right, so maybe she had been in a bit of a bad mood, but that was all because of that arrogant twerp who'd been doing up his shoelace and been giving her the eye. He deserved a punch, with his fancy waistcoat and smug face, and she'd been glad to deliver it. She only hoped she didn't bump into him again; heaven knows what his reaction would be this time. She would make sure she avoided him.

She pushed open the swinging door, and sent Daniel flying. His papers (actually, Harry's papers) scattered all over the floor. He'd been waiting right by the door so that she would send him, and them, flying. The bewildered Katie apologised to the back of Daniel's head as he scrabbled to pick up the loose papers. She offered to help.

'No!' shouted Daniel. His sharp response made her jump. 'No, I don't like other people to touch my notes.' Katie stepped back. Harry couldn't quite believe it; no wonder Daniel was keeping his face hidden from her. Surely he couldn't keep this up for long?

Katie was mortified, 'I'm so sorry.'

'They're strictly private.' Yes, thought Harry, you don't want her seeing them because she'll realise they're not yours. Daniel had now succeeded in collecting them, and was making neat piles.

Katie was desperate to make amends. 'I understand completely.'

No you don't, thought Harry. Daniel afforded himself a smile, unseen by his quarry.

'People should be more careful. These notes are my life,' he said.

'I know exactly what you mean.'

Daniel was warming to his performance – he was going the whole hog.

'How *could* you know?' He let it sink in – yes, enjoy the moral high ground while you've got it. He said, 'They're all I have. They're like ... ' What were they like? ' ... precious jewels.'

Harry was used, after years of art therapy, to not laughing out loud in delicate situations, but he had to bite hard on his lip. Precious jewels?

Katie hugged her briefcase to her chest. 'I feel the same way about my work.' Daniel collated his papers, caressing them. 'Look, if there's anything I can do ... ?' offered Katie.

'Dinner?' He'd gone for it, and he stood up triumphantly, having put his glasses on for that extra bit of attractive vulnerability.

'Anything at all,' she continued, then suddenly she realised. 'What?' She saw his face for the first time.

Proudly he repeated himself. 'How about dinner?' he said in best Roger Moore style. Katie cottoned on, and this time it was his chin that her fist struck. DOOF!

Daniel slumped, dazed, into Harry's arms, and was

22

dimly aware of Katie walking off. Ouch! Daniel rubbed his chin, looking to Harry for an explanation, but Harry grinned and commented drily, 'I see an autumn wedding.'

Katie was livid. How dare he ask her out on a date just like that! The arrogance, the insensitivity! What made him think she'd want to go out on a date with him! Or indeed with anyone whose only acquaintance had been a kick in the stomach and some scattered papers! And he'd deliberately sent them flying all over the floor. She could see that now. Her temper was not helped by the fact that her knuckle was somewhat painful. Not unpractised at punching men, she seemed to have hit this one particularly hard, and now her hand was feeling it. Never mind, she thought, she'd enjoyed it, and the look of horror and astonishment on his face had been worth it.

She headed out of the building, glad to be free of its ghosts of muttering, yawning scientists and lascivious designer-waistcoated would-be Romeos. Why were people so base? What mattered was research, intellectual rigour, informed conversation.

'All right, Dr Burrill – how about a quick one – drink, I mean?' She was passing the pub where Lloyd Park and Bill Something (Lloyd still didn't know and thought it rude to ask) were whetting their lunchtime whistles. He had only meant a drink; she looked rather lonely striding along with a heavy briefcase and furrowed brow. Lloyd was staggered at how much more a pint cost than in Cardiff, and wondered how they could justify the extra. It certainly wasn't for service. 'We could discuss S 1762 G4 or whatever his name is.'

Katie stared at this specimen of twentieth-century man with a look that was better described, not as 'if looks could kill', but 'if kills could look'. But she saw he was harmless. At least she knew where he was coming from. From a pub where men drank beer. She walked on by. 'Cheer up, it might never happen,' were Lloyd's parting words, whereupon he drained his glass and looked to Bill for further succour.

Katie got on the tube. She didn't have a car – let alone a flashy convertible. Palaeontological academia didn't pay as well as crypto-psychology. She looked around the half-empty carriage. They were all men, some were reading, some were just staring, and they all took varying degrees of interest in this new, female, arrival. She saw a free seat, and was about to sit down when an innocent young man on the other side of the aisle smiled at her. Katie moved on down the aisle, passing a black man engrossed in *Cosmo*.

This was Nigel Johnson, and he'd bought it because the front cover announced 'Top Ten Sex Tips'. Once he'd started looking at the women's magazines section in the newsagent, he'd spent several minutes deliberating between the various covers, all advertising something equally salacious. He'd been sorely tempted by the headline 'Ryan Giggs – Why We Can Win the European Cup', but had gone for *Cosmo*. Nigel didn't wear designer-label clothing, and worked for Edwards Premier Banking.

Katie moved on, past a man reading the *Sun*, who glanced up at her. Terry Atkinson had blond hair and a beige denim jacket. He gave her a quick inspection while chewing gum, and flashed a smile, which she ignored. He'd once seen an American film in which Ben Gazzara had got on a bus, flashed a woman a smile, she'd returned it, then given him a nod when she got off the bus: he'd followed her to her house and they'd had voracious sex. He'd often fantasised about this happening to him, but he'd never dared follow any woman, and had concluded that late sixties bohemian San Francisco was not the same as the Northern Line in the mid-nineties. He went back to his

Sun, and the article 'Ryan Giggs – Why We Can Win the European Cup'.

Katie moved on and sat between Terry Atkinson and a man with a friendly face and little round glasses, totally immersed in his book, *The Incoherence of the Incoherence*. Of him not much was known, except that he wore a skull-cap.

After a couple of pints, Bill Something and Lloyd Park returned to the subject of Dr Burrill, and the stultifying nature of her lecture. Bill blamed the lack of tonal variation, pace, graphics, and working models. Lloyd had another explanation, 'She's obviously a virgin.' Bill nodded sagely, though he couldn't quite see the relevance.

Katie had food shopping to do. Cullens was the most convenient but she resented the high prices they charge, and was glad that a Harts the Grocer had opened up nearby in direct competition for the lazy shopper, or the shopper who could only go late at night, or the single person for whom trips to the supermarket had to be rationed since they couldn't eat the amount of food necessary to justify the trip before it went past its best before date. Katie was in the last category, and she hated to waste food, but it was difficult when a lot of things came in packets of two, so you either had to be very greedy at one meal, or eat the same thing two days running, which was very dull. So she ate a lot of pasta. Sometimes she made sauce, sometimes she used bought sauce, either the stuff you got in supermarkets, or the more expensive, tastier sauce she got from the local deli, which was more likely to go off after having been opened. Sometimes she got their pesto (though only if she wasn't likely to be seeing anyone for a day, because the amount of garlic they used was verging on the criminal) and sometimes their red sauce.

Today she went to the corner shop, where the owner always asked how she was, really wanting to know why such an attractive woman never seemed to have a boyfriend, to pick up bread and milk, and then to Positano, the deli. She bought some fresh pasta, and some red sauce which Mrs Positano (Katie didn't know her real name, and even if she had done, would still have thought of her as Mrs Positano) had made to a new recipe, and wanted Katie to let her know if she liked it.

She walked along her street in Belsize Park. Her mother described it as Hampstead, others talked of Primrose Hill, but she was quite happy to stick with Belsize Park. Or Chalk Farm. She was weighed down by plastic bags of shopping and by thoughts of her day.

As she approached her front door, she heard a telephone ringing. She knew it was her own. She lived on the first floor of a Georgian terraced house, and fumbled to get the front door of the house open, then ran up the stairs, not easy with bags of shopping. She juggled her keys, and opened the door of her flat. Thankfully the phone was still ringing. She rushed through the door, shedding her mac, hat, briefcase and shopping, grabbed the phone, and fell into the armchair.

'Hello?' she said into the phone, still breathless from the climb up the stairs. It was a bad line. An operator spoke in Hindustani in the distance. She knew it must be Sandip. Indeed the operator confirmed that the caller was a Dr Tamar. Getting to a phone in the middle of the Punjab was not easy, so she had been eager not to miss the call, as he often rang her at home. 'Hello,' she repeated.

'Hello, Katie? Do you have a pen?' Sandip didn't waste time with social niceties. She liked that. Like her, he was totally dedicated to, and thoroughly fascinated by, his work. She held the telephone to her ear with her shoulder and picked up a pen and paper.

'Go.' She knew he must have exciting news.

'New find. Skeletal fragments. Fossilised. Female.' Katie scribbled: this was just the kind of breakthrough that could net them the grant for which they'd waited so patiently.

'Almost total erosion of skull.' She wanted to know it all straight away, and Sandip was letting her wait for each morsel of information.

'Dental structure?' she asked. That could tell them a great deal.

'Incomplete. But I think I've detected minute traces of carbon.'

Katie stopped taking notes, her mind turning over the possibilities this new opportunity presented. As she mulled them over, she whispered, 'Carbon in the teeth . . . cooked food.'

'Katie, this one liked her steak well done.'

She was delighted by this news. 'That's fantastic. Congratulations.' She could tell that Sandip shared her smile, thousands of miles away.

'What do you want to call it?' he enquired.

Katie had no hesitation. 'S 1762 G5. What else?'

'Of course.'

Sandip had been her supervisor when she was doing her postdoctoral thesis. She had had to fight hard to get him as he was much in demand and had little time to spare from his own research in India. But she had written a very persuasive letter, and had worked very hard for her interview with him. He had to tell her that even if he could take her on, which he very much doubted, she may spend months frustrated while he continued his own work on the Indian subcontinent. But Katie had been determined. She knew Dr Tamar to be a world authority.

He had proved invaluable to her, and had even recommended her for extra funding when she'd most needed it. His comments and suggestions had helped her shape her thesis, and he had even let her in on some of his own discoveries. He was much impressed by her work and her attitude, so that when he was looking for a new member of his team it was natural that he chose her, even ahead of others with more experience. She was able to begin work for him, and somehow her work and his coalesced, so that when she handed in her thesis, she knew that she owed him much of the credit even though the name on the front of it was hers. She was repaying him now, working hard on a project that bore his name, but on their latest application for a research grant from a private body they shared equal billing.

Katie's love life was another matter. Currently it veered between being non-existent and a little perfunctory dating when she decided she ought to have some romance. She was quite content to be single, and the long periods of celibacy didn't feel like a great sacrifice – more like an escape, really, until questions began nagging at her that maybe, just maybe, she was missing out. Her work was fulfilling and all important, leaving little time for anything else, but part of her knew there was still room for something extra. That something wasn't easy to find. Yes, she wanted someone who was her intellectual equal, but that didn't mean jumping into bed with the first palaeontologist she met at a conference. As this was, quite often, precisely what they had in mind, several conferences were graced with presentations from speakers with bloody noses or large band-aids on their chins.

She kept up with old friends – a school friend who had a husband and child would often try to set up dinner parties with eligible men, from which the eligible men would have to retire hurt. The friend gave up on her.

Of the men she'd been out with of late, none had got past the first date. Then there was Ashley. He had a degree in law, but hated law and lawyers. He'd started at Bar school but had left after two weeks as it was too horrendous, got a job in Madrid in financial journalism, and had recently returned. He really wanted to be a gentleman farmer, but couldn't figure out how to get into it. He was fascinated by Katie's work, but she wasn't fascinated by him.

Then she'd had a rest. But Pete had come along. He was something in publishing – selling probably, she thought – and he had to go to Frankfurt a lot, even though he spoke no German. He was a keen golfer, and when he told her his handicap was only five, she was unimpressed, but not nearly as unimpressed as he was when she asked what a handicap meant. Unfortunately, he'd taken it upon himself to answer this question, details of which, like 'stroke index', sounded interesting initially, but in the end meant that Katie had to leave before coffee.

Another time she'd gone to a dinner party where she knew a friend was trying to set her up. Unfortunately, Katie had forgotten which one was meant for her, and it was only halfway through the evening that she realised the one she had thought was 'hers', and sort of fancied, was, in fact, gay and was interested in the one meant for her, who was in turn interested in her, but she wasn't in him, and when the time came for after-dinner mah-jong they all left hurriedly.

Right now, Katie wanted to know more from Sandip.

'Are there any other signs? Was she part of a tribe?'

'We've checked. I don't think so. It looks like she dined alone.' That was all he could give her for the time being. More would be forthcoming later, but he'd be able to bring samples over in person soon, as he was coming over, hoping to hear more about the grant they'd applied for. Without it their work might be in jeopardy, but Sandip wouldn't even consider such an eventuality.

They said goodbye, and Katie set about her evening, buoyed both by Sandip's discovery and his impending visit. She looked at the pasta and sauce. Should she cook all of it? No – half tonight – half tomorrow.

Her flat consisted of a large living room dominated by french windows, a small bedroom, and a tiny kitchenette. This was estate agent parlance for 'a hob and a sink in a cupboard'. But that suited her fine. She generally dined alone, and didn't entertain much.

The french windows gave on to a little balcony, just big enough for one chair, where one could sunbathe, but Katie never did; she was far too demure.

Below lay the communal gardens, to which Katie was allowed access, but it meant having to go downstairs, out on to the street, along the road, round the corner, and in through a rusty gate, to which she had a key. She rarely ventured out there. The last time had been when there had been a 'jolly', when all the people who 'owned' the gardens (Katie paid a small but significant charge every month) got together with a barbecue, a tombola, a few sad-looking stalls and a paddling pool for the toddlers. She had been drinking some Pimms that had rather too much fruit in it, so that she ended up with mint leaves up her nose, when this man she recognised came up to talk to her. He lived on the other side of the gardens. She'd seen him put out his washing on his tiny balcony. Apart from the fact that this wasn't allowed, the contents of his washing was profoundly offensive. Underwear and tee-shirts that should have been pensioned off years ago to furniture-polishing duty were still being washed and called upon for wearing.

The thought of ever seeing him sporting the offending articles made her go quite cold with horror, but this prospect, she could tell, was the very thing on his mind as he approached her. After his seemingly innocent gambit of, 'Hallo, I'm Mark, I've seen you sitting on your balcony,' Katie walloped him, and had to leave in a hurry, eschewing even the Scotch eggs so lovingly created by Mrs Hancock at number ninety-six.

Thereafter she didn't feel able to go out on her balcony for three months, and had, indeed, often spotted him with his black eye, putting out his tasteless washing, almost in defiance of her as he stared angrily at her window, trying to catch a glimpse of his assailant.

As she prepared her meal she kept herself occupied with computer Scrabble and computer chess. These were her companions, and they didn't need catering for. Just before she served her pasta, she triumphantly put 'iota' into the portable Scrabble machine, which, while dramatic, kept the board closed down, and, as she told the computer just before pouring her meal out of the saucepan on to the plate, 'Note the double word score.'

She took her plate and the computer over to the sofa, by which time her disembodied opponent had made its response, and proudly beeped to let her know. 'Damn, that's quick,' she observed as she sat down. She looked at the word – spinster – and with a smile, retorted, 'Beating me is one thing. Calling me names on the other hand ... I'm deducting ten points for rudeness.' She flung the machine down and took a forkful of pasta, turning her attention to the computer chess. 'Get a move on. Thinking time's up.' Another forkful of pasta. She'd be glad to tell Mrs Positano how good the sauce was. The computer chess gave a beep to show that it had made its move. 'Thank you,' she responded affectionately. She'd always felt more at home with machines, with their lack of emotional complications, than with people.

She was still playing both games hours later as she lay in her white Victorian brass bed with curly bits. The Scrabble computer had just come up with 'milt', which, as the computer (but not Katie) knew, was the word for fish sperm. 'What? Never heard of it,' adding with mock menace, 'I can always look it up.' The chess game bleeped, signifying it had made its demon move. 'My knight! You took my knight.'

She looked hard at the board, and shook her head before announcing disconsolately, 'Damn! Mate in three moves – you're too good for me.' She held up her hands in surrender, turned her bedside light off and put her head down.

Chapter Three

Daniel spent the evening at Harry and Caroline's. He tended to do this once a fortnight or so, depending on how 'involved' he was. With them he could just relax – he didn't have to worry about body language, or control. The three of them – or four of them, now, with the arrival of Clare – would sit in the kitchen and Harry and Caroline would tease Daniel. Daniel loved it. These two, more than anyone else, knew his foibles, his pomposity, his immaturity, and he envied them their warm and solid relationship. Whenever he left their flat to go home, he'd feel a great twinge of regret that he hadn't yet found his soul mate. Sometimes he was able to persuade himself that the perfect partner didn't exist, and even if she did, then *he* certainly wasn't anyone's perfect partner – he was always destined to be the best man, never the groom, always the uncle, never the dad.

At their wedding Daniel had excelled himself with his speech, explaining how he had seen his stolid, sensible, mature friend Harry turn into a gibbering, poetic, romantic teenager within a week of being introduced to Caroline. He'd even kept one of Harry's letters at the time, which he read out as Harry hid under the table. 'Dear Daniel, Why did you wait so long to introduce her to me? She is fantastic. Please tell me that this sort of ex-boyfriend who is on the scene is definitely ex. I want her babies.'

Then, as Caroline joined Harry under the table, Daniel recounted her first comments about Harry to him. 'He is gay, isn't he? He wears pink shirts, and does art therapy and talks about you a lot – he must be gay.'

Daniel explained how he'd had a dinner party and invited them both, and they'd gone into the kitchen to do the washing-up after the main course, and hadn't emerged till everyone else had left. They'd spent the whole time chatting and giggling, without even touching the dessert spoons they were meant to be washing in the first place.

They spent this particular evening, as with many before, discussing Daniel's love life, with Daniel telling them first how irritating Lucy was – always insisting on going in the shower first, then taking for ever and leaving wet footprints on the bathroom floor, and what a bad driver she was; then telling them how much he'd miss her – her sparky sense of humour, her adorable nose and sexy eyes. Caroline and Harry looked at one another during the evening, knowing that they'd heard much of it before.

When Daniel got bored with his own stories he'd leap to the floor and play with little Clare. He'd loved playing with her ever since she was a baby, pretending he was teaching her the importance of strong and sustained eye contact in the social interface, but every time so much as a smile crossed her face as he went, 'Goo-goo, brrr,' he felt a sense of achievement unrivalled by any amount of serious nodding or applause from the businesspeople at his seminars. Now Clare was five, she was talking, and Daniel amused himself and her by teaching her words way beyond what she might pick up at nursery school. She couldn't quite get her tongue round 'solipsism' or 'insouciant', but had coped with 'didactic' and had shocked her teacher when using it in the playground.

As Harry swigged from his wineglass, and Caroline finished an apple, Daniel was kneeling under the table, playing with Clare, tickling her and pretending to bite her.

Caroline leant down to warn her daughter, 'Watch this one, Clare. Especially now he's single again. He'll eat you for breakfast.'

'Is my reputation that bad?' enquired Daniel as he prepared to dig his fangs into the giggling child's leg.

'Nothing compared to the truth,' muttered Harry as he took another sip of wine.

'Are you going to eat me for breakfast?' asked the little one, in delighted mock terror.

Caroline toyed with a grape, and observed to her husband, as if talking about a confused teenager, 'Look, if he's not ready to settle down yet . . .'

Daniel's indignant face appeared above the table, 'But I am.'

' . . . then there's nothing you or I can do to help him.'

'Owwh!' yelled Daniel, and ducked under the table to reprimand Clare. 'Don't bite, monkey!'

Clare was enjoying herself, 'Daddy, says you're a flirt.' Really, thought Daniel, and decided to get his own back for all the teasing he'd had from Harry about the pre-pre-foreplay represented by the punch in the gob. He leant down to whisper in Clare's ear.

Harry reached behind him, and picked up Daniel's painting from earlier in the day; he'd smuggled it home without Daniel's knowledge. He unscrunched it and showed it to Caroline. 'What do you make of this?' he asked, biting into an apple.

'It looks a bit like a child cast adrift on an endless ocean.'

Bang! Daniel bumped his head as he tried to get up from under the table to defend himself. Once he'd knelt up though, he couldn't think of any defence.

Then Clare popped up and announced to her father, 'Uncle Danny says you've got a very small penis.'

A lump of apple flew out of Harry's mouth and landed

on Daniel's painting. Like a child cast adrift on an endless ocean with a bit of apple floating nearby, thought Daniel.

'Bedtime,' announced Caroline firmly.

Caroline had known Daniel since their days at Durham University. They had both been at Collingwood College, which, unlike some of the others, had been mixed. She did English and Daniel did psychology. They'd met fairly early on – on the morning after the Freshers' Disco, where neither had scored and didn't know whether to be jealous of or repulsed by those that had – and had been great friends ever since. Friends. They'd never had a romance, possibly because Caroline could never take Daniel seriously as a lover. She was the sort Daniel would have gone for – slim and blonde with deep brown eyes – but he'd never really tried. She giggled at him too much, she knew too much about him, his fickleness, his manipulativeness, his immaturity, but also his qualities as a friend. He was loyal, and very open with her – even when recounting tales of what a twerp he'd been. And in return, Caroline never judged him, just gave him a friendly tap of admonishment.

She was much more of a steady ship on the romantic seas than him. She'd had a regular boyfriend in their second year at university. Lawrence was an oarsman who studied physics at Hatfield College, an all-male institution. He was initially suspicious of Daniel, but as time passed and his relationship with Caroline cemented, and Daniel went through a succession of mismatched and ill-fated relationships, he could see that Caroline was inured to Daniel's romantic charms.

The two men became great friends, which pleased Caroline apart from the odd occasion when they became too 'boysy' together. There was the time when they'd met in the college bar for an early drink and by mid-evening were in the sort of state in which stupid things seem reasonable. They decided to catch a train to nearby Newcastle, because they'd heard Sting was in his home town making a movie, and they wanted to go and meet him, and ask him what the lyrics of the song 'De Do Do Do Do De Da Da Da' really meant. Daniel had a theory that it was related to the Marxist concept of the rate of exploitation of labour, which Sting had now updated to embrace the notion of luncheon vouchers. Lawrence thought it was the noise Sting made when having an orgasm. Suffice to say, they didn't find Sting, but looked in every nightclub, restaurant and hotel they could, having a drink in each. When last orders came they wanted more alcohol, so decided to check in to the nearest hotel, where they could order drinks on room service.

By some unexplained quirk of late-night fate, they had an entourage with them: a man who said his name was Grub, but would give no further explanation, who could, and regularly did, recite the alphabet backwards, and claimed to have lived next door to Alan Gowling, the former Newcastle and Manchester United striker, and who, like most men in Newcastle, even in the depths of winter wore only a tee-shirt (and trousers, obviously, though not jeans); a bloke called Phil, who said virtually nothing but proceeded to consume most of the mini-bar, including the jar of cashews, the entire Toblerone and all the boiled sweets; and Jessica, a girl with hair permed to look like a fright wig, who worked as a waitress in a brasserie called Deans, themed on James Dean, where you could get a Giantburger, Rebel Without a Cause Chicken, or East of Eden Salad. It had been empty apart from Lawrence and Daniel, who had asked her if she'd like to come with them to a nightclub. She had agreed immediately, turned the sign on the door to 'closed', and sauntered into the kitchen only to emerge with Phil and Grub, much to Daniel's disappointment, because he'd thought he might be in with a chance. He kept trying to work out if Jessica was 'with' Phil or Grub. He didn't want to make a move because he reckoned that, though Phil might not say much, he could probably hit very hard. The mystery was cleared up, when, at four in the morning, with the mini-bar in ruins, Jessica left. Grub and Phil insisted on staying for continental breakfast, which would be served in the room if you filled in the little hanging menu and left it on the doorknob outside. When the stale croissants and lumpy rolls arrived at six, Lawrence, Daniel and Grub were asleep (Grub in the bathroom), and Phil ate the lot before departing, helping himself to the notepad and pencil provided on the bedside table, as well as the plastic shower cap from the bathroom.

Later that night, sitting in Clare's bedroom, Daniel told her and Caroline a bedtime story. It was about two yellow teddies, mainly so that Daniel could demonstrate with Clare's cuddly kissing bears. It had the desired effect, because before they had reached the Wizard of Brrreeeeeen, Clare was asleep. Caroline tucked her in.

Getting back to the subject of Daniel's love life, she whispered, 'Maybe you should see someone who's more of a challenge for you.' Daniel didn't respond; he just played with the bears, so she continued, 'I know that goes against the grain for a control freak.'

'Not at all,' he blurted, and Caroline had to shush him. 'It's just a question of finding someone who understands the real me.'

Caroline sniggered. The real? Teenage psycho-tosh. 'There are always dating agencies,' she suggested.

'The reject shop? Come on. They're strictly for losers. Desperadoes. No-hopers. Fourth Division relegation material.' Daniel was a little out of touch with the changes in the Football League. He may have vaguely heard of the Premiership, but wasn't aware that something with such a funny name could be the thing in which the top clubs in the country competed.

Caroline moved away and turned off Clare's bedside light. 'Losers, eh? Thank you very much,' she muttered as she walked out of the room. Daniel got up and followed her, anxious to make amends for his *faux pas*.

'Now hang on, you didn't meet Harry through an agency. *I* introduced you. In fact you said that they'd fixed you up with nothing but dorks.' Daniel had often wondered what the derivation of dork was. At school the boys who used to smoke behind the bike sheds had used it a lot (in fact, there wasn't room behind the bike sheds, because they were flush against a fence, and also right outside the staff room), assuming it to be rude, along with another favourite word, dopper. Daniel had yet to come across the latter in civilised society, but was hopeful.

Caroline stopped in the doorway and turned to Daniel, 'But I'd been signed up for months before I met Harry. For me it was a way of proving that I was serious.'

'Proving? Who to?'

'Myself.' She smiled and squeezed his nose for good measure.

As Daniel drove home, he pondered Caroline's suggestion. 'Myself, myself,' he repeated irritably. He'd never considered dating agencies. But perhaps this was the way to eliminate the unsuitable candidates – he could find out in advance what they were like, rather than having to go through the expensive and time-consuming process of dinner and so on before discovering they were weird or couldn't have a conversation without giggling every five seconds or were fans of daytime TV. Yes, he was quite keen, he could do all sorts of research beforehand. But what if someone recognised him? Ah, but the only person who could know was someone who was signed up with the agency themselves, who could hardly blurt it out in mixed company without having to explain their own involvement. It seemed foolproof, but he'd have to make sure no-one he knew saw him going to the agency's office. he could wear a hat: he never wore a hat normally.

He put his foot down so he could get home and have a good look through phone directories and magazines to find the best one. Unfortunately, just as he did, he went through a traffic light as it went from amber to red. He zipped by, oblivious, until a traffic cop on a motorbike, blue light flashing, flagged him down. 'Shit. Not again,' thought Daniel, as he pulled up. There was no Mothercare nearby, and as she got off her bike and took off her helmet, he realised it was the same cop, who wouldn't believe two births in two days, even with the advances made in fertilisation techniques, so he slipped Bruch's violin concerto into the car stereo.

When she reached his car, she found a different man, sullen, hunched over the wheel, pale and shaking, his voice cracking as he talked. 'I'm sorry, officer.'

'Did you know that light was red when you went through it?'

'No,' was all he could muster, staring at the dashboard, a forlorn figure.

'Don't you look at traffic lights before you go through them?'

'Yes,' his face draining of any life.

'Are you all right?' The cop was getting worried.

'Fine,' he croaked, before taking a deep, dismal breath. 'It's just . . . ' He began to sob gently.

'What is it?' asked the policewoman, trying to think if she had a paper hanky in her trouser pocket.

'I . . . please . . . I'm sorry . . . it's just my father . . . he's not well.'

'That's terrible. Just when the baby's been born as well,' she said, a croak now appearing in her voice.

'What? Oh yes, the baby. Yes, and he hasn't even seen him, he's been so ill. And we named him after him.'

'What's he called?'

'Who?'

'Your father – and the baby. It's the same, isn't it?'

'Yes . . . they're called, umm, Oliver,' so distraught with grief was he, that he could scarcely remember the name of his newborn son. 'I was on the way to see Dad. I suppose I was thinking about the life-support machine when I should have been thinking about the traffic lights. But, of course, you'd better do your duty, take me down to the station, but if I could just make one phone call.'

The cop could bear it no longer. 'Where is your dad?'

'In the hospital.'

'Yes, but which one?'

'Umm . . . the one nearby . . . the 'err, Royal.'

'The Royal Free?'

'Yes, yes, that one.'

'OK, I'll take you there right now. I'll radio ahead, and they'll clear the route.'

'Yes, splendid. That would be good . . . I . . . I don't think there's much time.'

So off they set, with her riding ahead of him, going through red lights, overtaking on roundabouts, until they got to the hospital, and the cop stopped by a door, which Daniel presumed was the entrance. He parked the car, and ran to the door. 'I hope he makes it,' she called after him.

Daniel turned back, still maintaining his gravitas, 'Thanks.' The sliding doors opened for him and he ran in. As they shut behind him, the cop drove off. A nurse at reception asked if she could help.

'No, I'm just browsing,' he answered, as he thumbed through pamphlets on safe sex and fibre in the diet. He strode out again, once the motorbike engine faded away in the distance, and sauntered over to his car. He took a last look to check that the policewoman had gone, and drove off, his mind drifting back to how to find someone who understood the real him. Maybe an ad in the lonely hearts column might be safer? He could tell from the letter, or perhaps better from their voice, if it was one of those where you leave a message on an answering machine.

He pondered what his ad might say. 'Tall, good-looking professional seeks similar'. Very dull. 'Are you the woman for me? High achiever seeks high-class lady'. Terrible – makes her sound like a prostitute. 'Man with GSOH seeks woman for TLC'. A bit coy, and perhaps there might be some people out there who, like he did until he realised a lot of the entries used the abbreviation, would misread GSOH as gosh misspelt rather than an indication of a good sense of humour; and maybe he wanted more than tender loving care – he wanted CEE – a challenging, exciting equal.

He'd have to try another tack. 'Romeo seeks Juliet' – too obvious; 'Heathcliff seeks . . .' – he couldn't remember who Heathcliff sought; 'Tom seeks Roseanne' – too dangerous; 'Prince seeks Princess' – far too dangerous; 'Clyde seeks Bonnie' – maybe; 'Bill seeks Hillary' – tricky, what if he ended up with a Gennifer, or Paula, or . . .; 'John seeks Norma' – hmmm; 'Maida Vale Male seeks Maid', 'Little Venice man seeks little Venus'. No, no, this was leading nowhere.

Listing his interests might be useful: 'Restaurants, music, women . . . ' Oh, dear.

Then inspiration struck. Honesty. Yes, honesty: 'This is the first time I've used the lonely hearts column. Maybe it's the first time you've looked, probably not, because, hey, we all look, don't we, but this is the first time you'll be *really* looking, even though you didn't know it, because this ad is just for you. Yes, you. I've just recently split up. It wasn't a long relationship, but it meant a lot. But it wasn't going anywhere. I want someone who understands the real me. The real me who gets involved in relationships, then self-destructs them. I manipulate every woman I go out with, so that she falls in love with me, so that I can claim it's unbalanced so that I can manipulate her into leaving me. But not you, because you're different. And, hey, maybe so am I. No longer a child cast adrift on an endless ocean, but a man seeking a woman, a soul mate, a life partner, a Challenging, Exciting Equal. Maybe it goes against the grain for a control freak like me, but I'm serious. Yes, this time I'm serious. No dorks, please.'

When he got home, he wrote this down. With that number of words, it would cost over a hundred quid. The dating agency would cost less. He'd go tomorrow. In a hat. Besides, it might help him stop constantly thinking about the woman who'd punched him twice. Yes, she was beautiful, but that gave her no right to punch him just for looking. And smiling. He wondered when she might next be at the Self Centre.

He screwed up the paper on which he'd written his putative ad. He was restless. He put on a CD – the 'Dies Irae' from Mozart's *Requiem*. He looked at his watch, it was a bit late, but stuff it, he turned it up very loud and began conducting the imaginary orchestra. His style was a little unorthodox: less like conducting, more like punching the air like a crazed boxer fighting someone eight feet tall, occasionally head-butting his opponent's knees. He found that, when a particularly violent section of music came up, he could clearly see his female assailant's face, and punched the air with defiant ferocity.

He cut an amusing figure as he stood in the middle of his flat, now in his shirt and waistcoat, gesticulating furiously. His flat was neat and tidy as usual, thanks to Mrs Gonzalez, his Colombian cleaning lady, who came Mondays and Fridays, and dusted, hoovered, ironed and did whatever needed doing, and tried to add a few feminine touches here and there. A vase of delphiniums stood on the sideboard as a monument to her continuing efforts to add something organic to the atmosphere.

The walls were red; a warm, African red, the interior designer had said, that would work both in winter and summer. The expanses of this warmth were broken up by the occasional picture – a carefully framed minimalist print or geographical drawing – and subtle up-lighting, illuminating bits of the wall and ceiling.

He imagined himself at a packed Albert Hall. The audience had never seen Mozart's work played with such aplomb. The London Symphony Orchestra were playing passionately, and the choir found almost heavenly inspiration from somewhere deep inside their diaphragms. It was a night to remember, and he didn't notice when someone walked up to his podium.

Lucy had let herself in. She'd shouted his name twice, with no response, before a third yell in his ear made him turn round. Lucy! His heart leapt! She was beautiful, he loved her sense of humour, he wouldn't mention her shower etiquette, or annoyingly diffident driving, and, best of all, he wouldn't have to go to any stupid dating agency wearing a hat.

He wondered whether to kiss her. No. Play cool at first, then mellow. Mention shower etiquette, then let her stay the night. He shouted over the music, 'Now look, if, and I stress *if*, you're going to come back there are some things we need to sort out.'

'My waistcoat,' she said, matter-of-factly.

Daniel was nonplussed. Waistcoat? Was that all she wanted? Not a reconciliation? That was hardly fair. The waistcoat suited him much better. He'd been wearing it for months. He'd assumed that in the 'divorce' settlement, he could keep the waistcoat and she could keep ... the memories of the good times, and that lettuce dryer that kept getting stuck.

He turned down the music with the remote control. Perhaps he'd misheard. 'I forgot my waistcoat,' she said, forcefully. Somehow the way she repeated 'waistcoat' hurt him rather. It seemed too businesslike. Love couldn't be reduced to mere clothes. Couldn't they talk about this like adults? He wearily took it off, and handed it over.

'I feel a lot better,' she reassured him. So she wouldn't be staying the night.

'I'm glad,' he croaked. She was covering up, she was heartbroken.

'You should be.'

'Well, I am,' he squeaked. What was this, she didn't want him back? Not that he would have her back, no, he was much wiser now, he knew it could never be, but he would let her stay the night if she needed to. He realised she'd been through a lot, and perhaps he could help her over it – no more, no less.

She handed his keys over. 'Do the world a favour, Daniel, sort yourself out.'

So she wasn't staying the night. Should he ask her? No, he had his pride, his integrity. She moved towards his face.

A kiss? He leant down, lips ready. She went for his cheek. Fine. She turned and went to the front door without looking back, and banged it shut behind her. Daniel watched her go. Thank goodness she hadn't wanted to stay the night. He sighed. It really was over. He was alone again. Good, he could start afresh, with a new, positive attitude. He looked at the front door. No knock. She'd have to knock, now she had no key. No knock came.

She'd seemed very calm, very relieved. Maybe she'd planned it. Maybe she had manipulated him? Now she was free to find someone else. Or maybe she'd already been having a thing? *Had* she been having an affair? With Bananaman? She'd said he sometimes had to change in very confined spaces at conferences and PR appearances. Had she helped him on with his yellow tights and it had gone from there? What was his name again? Clive? Philip? Howard? Something like that.

What about that night she didn't call from Keswick? She'd said it was a fruiterers' conference. How could he be sure? He'd never suspected anything. Why should he? She was the one who was jealous all the time. Perhaps he'd ring the Fruit Council or whatever and find out if they'd had a conference in Keswick in March. Or what about that dinner that had gone on so late? She'd said it was an awards ceremony – 'You won't enjoy it, I'll be rushed off my feet.' Oh, yeah. Rushed off her feet by some bloke from the Jalapeño Marketing Board. What was it again? Snacks Advertising Awards? At the Inter-Continental Hotel. He'd ring them tomorrow.

Why, though? What did he care now? He knew it was over. He was glad it was over. He'd wanted it to be over. He was an expert on manipulation. He taught businessmen to be confident, even to look slightly unsure if it helped. 'Incidentally,' he would say, with a grin, 'I've found this

46

particular stance, the slightly unsure look, works very well with women, too. As the French would say, it's more *sympathique*. If on the other hand you want a girl to leave you, the best thing to do is to stay silent until she realises that *she* wants to leave *you*.'

Last week, a man had asked what sort of body language he should use if he's caught cheating on his wife. Everyone laughed, except Daniel, who responded, 'Why should you want to cheat on your wife? Don't you love her? What I am teaching is control. Control is power. Lack of control equals loss of power. And cheating on your wife shows a complete lack of control. Cheating is for losers.'

Perhaps Harry knew if Lucy was cheating? Perhaps Harry had known all along about Bananaman and had never let on to protect Daniel. Daniel decided to put the kettle on. Well, she could have her Bananaman, or jalapeño gigolo! He was going to the dating agency tomorrow, and he'd have a date every night of the week soon. He'd play the field, he'd sample lots of hors d'oeuvres before deciding on his main course. Oh yes. And who was that woman today? What was she lecturing on? Fossils? He could find out her name from the Self Centre office, and where she worked. Punching someone twice was pretty extreme action. She obviously had something to cover up. She fancied him rotten. Like he fancied her rotten, with her little briefcase, endearing concern for his notes, and sexy ankles. Yes, he'd follow that one up. But not before signing up with a dating agency. Perhaps that was a safer way to find the real love of his life.

So, Operation Dating Agency. Should he give a false name? No, silly, could lead to complications later – and what about paying? Wouldn't do to sign up a Mario Rugoletti, and then pay with a cheque in the name of Daniel Becker. He'd need a hat to go there. He went to his wardrobe, and fished out the head apparel. There was a New

York Yankees hat made of corduroy which he had bought at a baseball game at Yankee Stadium. He'd proudly returned to his seat with it, only to be told by Harry that only nerds and hicks bought corduroy hats. Harry, as an American, had also insisted on bending the brim at the sides, to make it look less nerdy. This was a continual gripe for Harry, who, having actually managed to pick up the rules of cricket through careful watching of games on television and intensive questioning of Daniel, still failed to understand why the players didn't turn down the brim at the side. He thought they looked dorky, and took this opportunity to reduce the dork-factor in Daniel's corduroy hat.

Daniel was happy to let this happen, but felt safe in the knowledge that his headgear didn't look as stupid as that of some of the opponents' fans. The Yankees were playing the Milwaukee Brewers. Milwaukee is in Wisconsin, the Cheese State, so some of their followers were wearing large pieces of cheese on their head. This, Daniel felt, showed a loyalty somewhat beyond the call of duty. What they were sporting, quite openly, were large segments of plastic cheese about a foot long, with head-shaped moulds underneath for easy wearing.

Daniel had always been impressed by this labelling of states: New Jersey, the Garden State; California, the Golden State; Florida, the Sunshine State. He often thought it would be amusing if British counties did the same: Surrey, the Posh County; Warwickshire, Shakespeare's County; Devon, the Creamy County; Rutland, the Non-existent County; Avon, the County Nobody Wanted in the First Place Which is Likely to Disappear Soon; Worcestershire, the Saucy County; Gwynedd, the County with Two Ds; Northumberland, Sting's County; Sussex, the Sexy County; Caithness, the Rugged County; Kent, Gateway to Europe.

He rejected the baseball cap, and found a foldaway flat cap that he'd bought on holiday, when it had been very sunny and he didn't want to get sunstroke or spend much on a hat. It had a popper on the front, which unpopped to make the peak come away from the rest of the hat. When he wore it like this he could look like an extra from *Fiddler on the Roof*, or he could close the popper and look like his father on the golf course. He continued his search. Next he found a floppy hat, which, while suitable for lolling around the beaches of the Bahamas, or fielding at forward short leg, probably wouldn't look so good in central London on a grey day.

Then he thought he'd found the right answer – a trilby. Its large brim would cast a pleasingly mysterious shadow on his face. Excellent. He'd bought it when he had been doing a seminar in Cambridge. He'd been caught in the rain, and hadn't wanted to buy yet another of those silly little umbrellas that you buy when it's raining, which then spends the rest of its life living under a car seat or at the bottom of a shoe cupboard or hanging on a doorknob near the front door but which you always forget when you go out in the rain, so you end up buying another silly little foldaway umbrella with a twee floral pattern which you wouldn't be seen dead with unless it was raining.

So he'd gone into a gentleman's outfitters, where trousers are slacks, where the shopfront and lettering were done in 1953, where the assistants have tape measures round their necks and where Chaka Demus and Pliers aren't blasting from the sound system. In fact, there isn't a sound system. 'I'd like a hat, please,' he had boldly announced when approached by an assistant, twenty-two going on fifty.

'What sort of hat, sir?' enquired Martin, for that was his name, if the oblong badge on his lapel was to be believed.

'One to keep my head dry – how about that one?' Daniel said, pointing at a bottle-green trilby.

'Certainly, sir, what size are you?' This stumped Daniel. He offered his shirt size instead. This didn't help, so the tape measure was able to come into full effect, as Chaka Demus might have said.

'Seven-and-a-quarter, sir,' smarmed Martin, handing him the one Daniel had pointed out.

'Hmm,' said Daniel, looking at himself in the mirror.

Martin's reflection leant in with another. 'I think you'll find this will be more satisfactory, sir,' assured Martin. He was right, and so chuffed was Daniel that he kept it on while paying. 'Hats aren't worn much these days,' volunteered Martin, 'but they do look very distinguished. I've got one exactly the same as that, and everyone comments on it. Most favourably.'

Daniel nodded, as he looked at himself in his bedroom mirror. Yes, this would do.

Now to choose which dating agency. He called Caroline and Harry. They were asleep, so couldn't be that pleased with this development. Caroline told him the name of the place she'd tried – A1 Dates – although she couldn't really recommend it, and Daniel thought it sounded too much like a cab company. They groggily told him to try listings magazines, Sunday supplements and the Yellow Pages. He found a plethora. He was able to dismiss Love Hearts, Eros, Romance, Dreams Fulfilled, Computer Love, Astrological Amour, Lux Romantica, Baptist Spouse Hunters, Scorpio, Mah-jong Matrimonials, Opera Lovers' Lovers, and Partner Profiles. His shortlist included Personality, Attractions, Love at First Sight (But Only After Extensive Research), Matchmaker, and Discretion.

Chapter Four

The next morning he strode up to an old building in the Aldwych, not far from the splendid Waldorf Hotel, sporting the hat and a cream mac, an ensemble that made him look like a Humphrey Bogart-style private detective. Or so he hoped. The building housed Discretion, which he'd chosen because that seemed to be their major selling point. Approaching the front door, he glanced to check it was the right number, then walked on, anxious to ensure there was no-one he knew around. He stopped in a doorway and surveyed the scene. A man went into the building, balding, grey, fiftyish. A possible Discretion candidate, or perhaps he was heading for one of the other offices in the building.

Daniel looked around. There was a phone box. Should he call Harry? No. Caroline? No. They'd both tell him to go for it. And take that hat off. He could call Lucy – tell her he was very sorry, he'd sorted himself out, he loved her and would she come back? Tonight they'd celebrate – eight o'clock at Angelino's, his favourite restaurant.

No. Lucy was the past. Perhaps he could find out more about that palaeontology lecturer. No, he wanted a girlfriend, not a sparring partner. Just then a young woman stopped outside the Discretion building. Tall, with red hair, cowboy boots, jeans, leather jacket: attractive. Maybe she was for him. Daniel leapt from his hiding place, his eyes fixed on his possible target, and bumped into an old lady coming from the other direction with one of those shopping bags with wheels on the bottom. The red-head looked over, and Daniel smiled as he helped the lady compose herself. The red-head went in. Discretion-bound, no doubt. Daniel made sure the old lady was all right, then bounded after his quarry. He had to check which floor – fourth. He strode into the building. It had one of those old lifts, with a see-through grille door. The red-head was waiting for the lift. Daniel slowed as he approached her. She gave him a glance. He smiled. The lift came. He gallantly extended a hand, letting her go first, then jumped in behind her, making sure he got to be in charge of the buttons.

'Which floor?' he asked, nonchalantly pressing Four. 'Sixth, please,' came the reply.

'Pardon?'

'Sixth,' she reaffirmed, tetchily leaning over to press the Six herself.

'Oh. What happens on the sixth floor?'

'Simpson International Haulage. Why, what happens on the fourth?' He was trapped. Damn. If only he'd kept his mouth shut.

'Erm, Discretion. International . . . umm, private investigation unit.'

'It's a dating agency, isn't it?' she said, coolly.

'Yes. That's the cover though.' He attempted to appear mysterious. And failed. 'We mostly do industrial espionage cases, that sort of thing.'

'Well, you seem to get a lot of lonely-looking men going in there. They all wear hats and raincoats.'

'Operatives. Under cover. Disguise.' He was praying for the lift to reach the fourth floor. Unfortunately it stopped at the third. A middle-aged woman got in and pressed seven. At least it might mean Red-head would stop her interrogation. The lift ascended. Ding! Fourth floor – relief! The doors opened slowly. Daniel squeezed out. He thought about tipping his hat to the ladies. No, don't draw attention. He headed down the corridor, past a woman in a business suit. He kept his head down.

The lift door shut and the red-head shouted loudly after him, 'Hope you find a girlfriend, mister.' Aaargh! The Business Suit stared at him, the Ice Queen of WC2, and he smiled wanly in return.

He sauntered along the corridor, taking deep breaths, trying to regain his composure. Suddenly there was the door. DISCRETION, it said. Plain, simple and, above all, discreet. He rearranged his mac, folding the collar up and adjusting his scarf to afford maximum concealment. He opened the door and boldly stepped in. Nobody was in the outer office, but he could hear voices from the inner. It all looked fairly ordinary, with desks, filing cabinets and some pink and blue hydrangeas in a vase. He went up to the reception desk and peered nosily at a file. Behind him the door from the inner office opened and out came a middle-aged woman who eyed him suspiciously. Dorothy Oxford wore a purple blouse and pearls, with her glasses suspended over her stomach by a cord round her neck. She held a file in her left hand. She'd seen it all before.

Daniel offered a lame smile, putting one hand in his coat pocket and removing his hat with the other. 'Hi.' He felt relieved to have uttered a word, albeit a short one, and continued, 'I wonder if you can help me?'

'I doubt it.'

How many other men had she seen nervously standing there in their hats and coats? He grinned. She bade him sit down, and took out a form for him. She'd just made a pot of tea, and offered him a cup. He readily accepted. He decided that she would be a useful ally, and that if he could ingratiate himself with her, she would make sure that he'd get the pick of the crop, and none of the duds.

He slipped his glasses on, and when she returned with the tray of tea things, he offered to 'be mother'. She accepted, delighted by this charming, vulnerable young man. Once he'd poured the tea, she indicated the little sofa, and he removed his mac and sat down. As she was having a bit of a tea break, and she knew that her boss, Mrs Dwyer, would be some time with the client in the office, she sat beside him on the sofa, and they both sipped their tea.

Daniel was delighted by this and indulged in some subtle copy behaviour to win her over, crossing his legs when Mrs Oxford – 'Oh, please, call me Dorothy' – did, nodding when she did, tutting when she did and so forth. He told her his name, but insisted she call him Daniel, and recounted his tale of woe; how he hadn't met the right girl yet, how he wanted someone to understand the real him, how much he had to give, and how sad he was about the break-up with Lucy. Mrs Oxford warmed to him, and hoped that Mrs Dwyer's current client would take as long as possible.

'I can't believe she came back just to pick up her waistcoat,' tutted Mrs Oxford. Daniel mmmed in agreement, his mouth full of tea. 'Women can be so callous,' she continued.

Daniel was enjoying himself, and explained, 'So, you see, I'm just disenchanted.'

'You mustn't blame yourself,' she tried to reassure the poor poppet, putting her hand on his, and moving her face close to his.

'Well, I do,' said the poppet, touching her hand before removing his glasses and getting up, intrigued by the raised voices that were coming from the inner office.

Daniel wandered to the glass partition. He couldn't quite make out what they were saying, and couldn't see, because the glass was vertically bevelled, like the glass that

54

windows in school staffroom doors are made of, so that light can pass, but the children can't peer in and see where the music teacher keeps his sherry. He put his ear to the glass, but Dorothy was still talking. 'Look, I'll see if Mrs Dwyer can make an arrangement to see you as soon as Mohammed Ali leaves.'

Daniel sauntered over to the inner office door, vaguely recognising one of the shouting voices inside. 'Mohammed Ali?' His ear was fixed to the door when suddenly it opened and out came a woman. They came face to face. He looked at her. She looked at him. They recognised each other. It was Katie Burrill.

Thoughts zoomed through Daniel's mind: 'Oh, not just looking for pre-historic men, then? So our notes-obsessed palaeontologist does have hormones after all.' He shifted his weight, smiled and leant on the doorframe, and chucklingly said, 'Well, isn't this a surp–'

Bam! A hard right to the stomach, and she was gone, leaving Daniel again struggling to regain any semblance of dignity or breath. Mrs Dwyer saw what happened, and calmly announced, 'I'm so sorry. One of our ex-clients.' She gaily shut the Burrill (aka Mohammed Ali) file, and said to the heap on the floor, 'Won't you come in?'

Katie had been a Discretion client for six months now. She had realised that perhaps she needed something outside her work, and was afraid she'd end up lonely and bitter, but she couldn't afford to waste time 'dating' in the usual manner. Besides, if you want to buy a house, you go to an estate agent – so why not go to a dating agency for a companion? This way she could avoid some of the normal pitfalls of romance. But Mrs Dwyer didn't seem to understand what she wanted. Mrs Dwyer seemed to give much more emphasis to the physical side, and it had disquieted Katie when, on her second visit to Mrs Dwyer, she had seen Mrs Dwyer's Take That Fan Club membership card. She didn't know if it was quite seemly that a middle-aged woman should be a member of the fan club for a pop group of barely post-pubescent boys, but had caught them once on *Top of the Pops*, and had been slightly attracted to the one at the back with a sweaty chest.

Today Katie had come for a showdown. She'd arrived about half an hour before Daniel, determined to make Mrs Dwyer understand once and for all what she wanted. Mrs Dwyer said she, too, wanted to talk.

Mr Dwyer had died a few years previously, causing her great grief, but rather than become a lady of leisure she had invested her inheritance in this business, which was doing well thanks to her nose for a suitable match and her efficient, personable manner. She was a beautiful, well-groomed woman of fifty or so and had found new romance herself; she now lived with a thirty-five-year-old musician named Leslie. Her patience had been wearing thin with Katie, and she was glad of the chance to talk face to face.

'I'm sorry, Miss Burrill,' she began (Katie didn't like to use the Dr prefix other than in work situations, or communications with the telephone, gas, electricity or water companies; or when contesting parking tickets – it could be handy), 'but I think we just have to admit to failure in your case.' It was the first time such an admission had been necessary in eight years, but Katie was a unique case.

'But why?' pleaded Katie. Mrs Dwyer didn't answer. Not vocally at least. She opened Katie's file, and produced several polaroid photos of men – Katie's dates, all bruised or damaged in some way. Daniel was not unique. Others had been walloped or punched. As Dorothy Oxford, who was doing some filing in the corner, looked on and tutted, Mrs Dwyer laid out the photos (of Ashley, Pete and others) like exhibits at a trial. Once Dorothy had gone out to drink tea with Daniel, Katie defended herself. She felt she had to, and both women's tempers were becoming frayed. 'Don't you understand?' she asked. 'I'm looking for a man with *intellectual* passions. Maybe a man I can just have a friendship with.'

'A man you can just have a friendship with is only a lover you don't want to sleep with.'

Katie didn't want to go into that. She wanted to walk out and never see Mrs Dwyer again, but she had a point to prove. Her open palms tried to add emphasis to her argument. 'Look, all I'm saying is, it would be nice if you could arrange for me to meet someone who doesn't think with his genitals.'

This was a sharp dig, Katie hoped, at Mrs Dwyer's selection procedure, but the latter remained unruffled, and far from replying in kind with cheap jibes, tried to lift the conversation to a poetic level.

'Have you ever made passionate love on a sunny spring afternoon,' she enquired, a picture of Leslie in her mind, as Katie looked away embarrassed, 'with a cool breeze caressing your body and carrying your cries of ecstasy up beyond the trees?' She gave Katie a knowing look, hoping to bring out a scintilla of passion that may reside in her hard and rational mind.

Katie looked skywards, and cried, 'God save me from romantics.'

'I suspect he already has,' replied Mrs Dwyer, giving up any hope on this one, and mentally closing her file. 'Now if you don't mind.'

Katie's blood was boiling now. Why couldn't this woman understand and find her a man, her equal, someone interested in the finer things – someone like Sandip even, for whom intellectual pursuits were paramount?

She realised she was being dropped. 'You can't throw me out!'

Mrs Dwyer was now quite determined. She didn't want her agency to become an adjunct to the casualty ward. It was the first time she'd dropped a client, but this one really was different. 'Yes I can and I will. I'm only protecting my clients.'

'Have you ever wondered if they're worth protecting?'

'I'm sure you'll have a lot more fun playing computer bridge than kicking, thumping and punching every man on God's earth.'

That was it. Katie had to leave. Having one of her three hobbies, as confidentially mentioned on her application form (along with computer chess and computer Scrabble), thrown back at her was the last straw. She stormed to the door and wrenched it open, only to be confronted by Daniel. His smug face, his air of 'I know you fancy me' and unbelievably irritating observation, 'Well, isn't this a surpri–' could be treated in only one way. A hard right to the stomach. And off she strode to the lift, hoping to make a swift getaway.

She opened the outer grille door, got in and shut it. She pressed G for Ground, and the inner grille shut. Daniel emerged from the dating agency, still a little short of breath. Once he'd got up from the floor, and Dorothy Oxford had said, 'Mrs Dwyer will see you now,' he'd dashed out, managing only, 'I'm going to take on Mohammed Ali,' in response.

The lift was already descending when Daniel reached it. Katie's head was at about Daniel's knee height. He blurted, 'What ... Why do you keep hitting me?' Her head disappeared out of view. Daniel took the stairs. The lift shaft ran down the middle of the stairwell, so she could still hear him. 'I said – why do you keep hitting me?' Katie sighed. He surely wasn't going to run all the way down to the ground floor?

'Go away!'

Daniel was doing well, the age of the lift mechanism and his determination to tame this pugilist combining to help him keep up.

'What have I done?' he exclaimed. 'What's so special about me?'

'Don't flatter yourself.'

This took Daniel by surprise. He'd assumed, or hoped, that this proclivity for bashing him was eccentric – well, very eccentric – courtship display, or pre-pre-foreplay. Or she was potty. 'Oh, do you hit lots of people then?'

Katie shifted uncomfortably. She did, but why should she have to discuss it with this eager twerp?

'All the time,' she shouted, hoping finally to put him off.

But far from doing this, it intrigued him all the more. Here was a beautiful woman, clearly very bright and highly qualified academically, who succumbed to periodic bouts of violent delinquency. He'd got into a nice rhythm, and could take the steps at quite a pace now, without having to look.

'Are you popular?' he cheerily bawled.

No answer. Then a little noise – he couldn't quite make it out, but felt more sure than not that it was a 'no'.

'What?' he yelled, confident that he'd hit a raw nerve.

She was fed up. First Mrs Dwyer, now him. Well, she didn't care, and shouted back at him, 'No. I am not popular.'

'I'm stunned,' commented Daniel, now full of beans because he had the upper hand. He'd reached the ground floor before her and got her to make this admission.

'What?' she asked, not because she didn't hear what he

said, but because she realised she was about to reach the
bottom and he'd be there. She quickly pressed Stop, then
Four, and the lift obeyed. Daniel was standing proud and
relaxed, a bit like Superman, with hands on hips and feet
splayed, ready for her to walk into him. But then he
noticed the lift had changed direction.

'What did you do that for?' Off he went up the stairs
again.

'To avoid you. I don't want to see you and I don't want
to talk to you.' And she didn't want to have to punch him
again. Three times seemed enough.

Daniel was back in his stride again, in every sense. He
was easily keeping up with the lift, and felt he had won a
few small battles – after all, she was telling him about herself, and she could quite easily have told him to piss off.
Now was the time to press home his advantage. 'Does
that mean you won't have dinner with me?' He faltered
on a step, his legs beginning to give way.

'Yes . . . No!' came her reply. She was annoyed with
herself for losing sight of the syntax.

'We could sit at different tables if you like.'

'No,' she screeched, and pressed the Stop button again,
and then G. The lift descended. Daniel collapsed from ex-
haustion, but waited for the lift to pass him. He pressed
close to the grille, knowing he could catch her eye as she
went down. And he wouldn't have to shout.

'Angelino's? Eight o'clock.' She looked back at him, he
did at least deserve a bit of eye contact for all his efforts,
but that was all.

'No. I'm sorry.' And she was gone.

Daniel sat on the stairs, exhausted, trying to recapture
his breath. She'd looked at him. A warm look. 'I'm sorry,'
as well. This was encouraging. He was still puffing heavily
a few seconds later when the red-head came by, walking

down the stairs, having got fed up waiting for the lift. 'No luck then, mister?'

By the time he got to the Self Centre, Katie's 'No, I'm sorry' had become, for Daniel, a definite promise to be there. Of course she couldn't just say yes. She had to maintain some mystery, some allure, she couldn't be seen to be 'easy'. Yes, Daniel had seen it in her eyes. She'd be there. Daniel strode into Harry's office. Harry was in the darkened Therapy Room collecting paintings. Daniel opened the door, and proudly announced, 'Eight o'clock,' before shutting it behind him.

'What?' He must mean Katie Burrill – that was her name – Daniel had told it to him proudly and said he was going to try and find out more about her from the Centre office. That 'autumn wedding' crack had really got to him. But he surely hadn't got her to agree to a date already? Maybe Daniel had been right – perhaps those punches had been pre-pre-foreplay.

'Eight o'clock,' Daniel repeated from the other room. Harry rushed out of the Therapy Room with several paintings under his arm.

'Angelino's?' he asked, trying to see where Daniel was. He'd hidden behind the door, and with a grin that would have better suited a five-year-old who'd been given a year's supply of Bounty ice creams, popped out and confirmed it.

'The Usual, Harry,' and laughed a piratical laugh. Harry wasn't convinced – he'd seen the look on her face after the notes incident.

'She won't turn up.'
'She will.'
'She won't.'
'She will.'

'She won't.'

'She will.'

'She won't.' Harry held his hands up.

'She will.'

'She won't.'

Daniel put his face to Harry's. 'She will.'

'She won't.'

'She will.'

'She won't.'

'She will.'

Harry tried another tack. 'No way.'

But Daniel was sure, and he explained as Harry folded the paintings ready for the shredder, 'She'll be there, Harry. She'll be ten to fifteen minutes late,' Harry was mmming and nodding in mock agreement, 'just to leave me hanging on, to get me worried. But she'll be there.'

Harry whispered in his ear, 'She won't.'

Katie pondered what to do. She wasn't used to being pursued in this manner, and her pursuer obviously wasn't used to being repulsed in this manner. Perhaps she'd be doing womankind a service if she went out with this specimen, who clearly considered himself God's gift to the female race, and brought him down a peg or two. Yes, why not – she could show him that not all women would come under his spell. So she rang Discretion, told Dorothy Oxford it was her and asked for the name of the young man whom she'd punched. Dorothy was reluctant, unwilling to be an accessory in a GBH case, but Katie explained that he had invited her out for dinner, and she merely wanted to leave a message at the restaurant for him, because she might be late. Dorothy was concerned, 'He's a very delicate flower, you know. He's been badly hurt. He's just finished with a girlfriend and wants someone who understands the real him.' After a few more minutes of this, during which Katie reassured Dorothy that she would tread very carefully, Dorothy told her what she wanted to know. Daniel Becker.

She'd never been to Angelino's. It was far too expensive for her, or for the sort of person with whom she mixed. Her father could have afforded it, but it wasn't his sort of place. It was a fancy riverside restaurant. It had valet parking. She'd read about it in a Sunday supplement. It wasn't near a tube station. She'd have to get a taxi, at least some of the way. And what was she to wear?

Daniel wore his dark suit. Lucy had always liked him in it, and even without the waistcoat it looked good. As usual, he chose a white shirt, but which tie? A dark one with white splotches. They were designer splotches, of course. So, he was full of beans as he pulled up outside Angelino's. The building had once been a bank, and had impressive pillars at the front which gave on to a cobble-stone courtyard, which sloped down to the river. He left the car door open for the valet, who got in and drove it away. Daniel almost skipped into the restaurant, checking his watch on the way. One minute to eight.

He went up to the front desk, between two pillars, where the manager, Vincenzo, was sitting. He greeted Daniel effusively. 'Good evening, Signor Becker! *Come stai?*'

'*Tutto va bene.*'

Vincenzo got up to show Daniel to his table.

'*Bene. Bene. Multo bene?*' Vincenzo wanted to be on the safe side.

'*Sì, sì,*' Daniel reassured him, '*multo bene.*'

Once he had clarified that tutto was va-ing multo bene, Daniel had exhausted his Italian, so switched to English as they wandered through the restaurant. 'I want the very best of everything tonight.'

'*Sì, sì*. Always. I have the oysters your mother would die for.' He kissed his fingers to emphasise his point.

'Good,' said Daniel, then paused. Perhaps he would have to be more subtle with this one.

'No. No, no, no . . . Nothing too obviously romantic.'

'Ah. I understand. *Niente*. No oysters?'

'*Niente*,' Daniel repeated, stressing his words by cutting the air with his hands. 'No oysters. No asparagus. No figs. You get the picture. Not the usual. I need something . . . less certain.'

Vincenzo stopped him and offered, 'If I may make a suggestion . . . Why not offer the young lady the menu?'

'Brilliant! So she can decide for herself.' Great idea. Daniel was calm again. Why was he so on edge? He looked at his watch. 'Okay, now she should be arriving in five min–' But she was already there, sitting at what was obviously Signor Becker's table. She looked stunning and Daniel was stunned.

'Hello,' she purred, demurely, her hair slicked back, her lips reddened, wearing a sleeveless grey dress with a black cardigan that had slipped slightly to reveal enticing female flesh. She'd been there fifteen minutes, and thanks to Dorothy Oxford, knew exactly whose table to ask for. Fifteen-love.

Vincenzo pulled out a chair, Daniel sat and took a menu. He tried to regain his composure, quite undermined by her beautiful presence, and stuttered, 'I wasn't sure that –'

'– I'd come? Why ever not?'

Daniel thanked Vincenzo, grateful for his support, and rather scared now, face to face with his quarry. Barely had his hands taken the weight of the menu, when Katie barked, 'Are you ready to order?'

'Yeah, sure,' lied Daniel. He picked up his napkin:

things could get violent again and it could be handy if he got a nosebleed. Katie was in a hurry, clearly. She gestured to Vincenzo, who came running.

'Signorina?' Daniel was still fumbling with the menu and his napkin, each vying for a resting place on his lap.

'What's the best thing on the menu?' she asked.

Vincenzo proudly began to tell her, 'It is all –'

'– I know. But what's the *best* thing? What does Signor Becker usually have?' Vincenzo looked at Daniel, who was lost for words.

'Usually?' mused Vincenzo, trying to play for time.

'Usually,' she repeated, staring at Vincenzo, then at Daniel.

'Well, err . . .' flailed Vincenzo, looking at her, then at Daniel.

'I tell you what,' she announced. 'We'll have the asparagus. Followed by the oysters.' She paused, to smile sweetly at her escort. 'Is that all right?'

'Perfect,' Daniel grinned meekly. Thirty-love.

'And to drink?' ventured Vincenzo.

Daniel felt he had to attack, so answered immediately, a tad too loudly, so as to stop Katie getting in first. Sancerre was his choice, and hers, it seemed.

'You took the word right out of my mouth,' she said. Vincenzo smiled, took the menus, and walked away.

Now they were alone, Daniel could launch a charm offensive. He leaned over and chuckled, trying not to appear the nervous fourteen-year-old he felt, 'We must have very similar tastes.'

She smiled back, and enquired, 'So . . . why are you interested in having a date with me?'

Daniel raised an eyebrow, just a touch. She was direct. But at least she wasn't punching him. He prepared to speak, his palms open in the please-I-beg-you-to-believe-me-it-hurts-but-it's-true mode.

'Well, I've always been looking for a serious, steady –'

'– Girlfriend,' she interrupted. 'Have you?'

'Yes, of course. You see, it's just that I can't seem to get the balance –'

'– Right in a relationship.'

She did it again. Perhaps she could understand the real me, thought Daniel.

'Exactly,' he said. 'It's not that I don't try. Somehow everything works for a while, and then I find –'

'– That you get tetchy and frustrated.'

This was weird, felt Daniel, and verging on the irritating. He continued, 'Almost –'

'– Deliberately.'

'That's right.' He sat back. He wanted to punch her now. Couldn't she at least let him have his moment of openness, honesty and vulnerability without butting in and spoiling his poignancy? He leant forward with what he hoped appeared to be a good-natured chuckle, 'Do . . . Do you always –'

'– Finish off people's sentences? Yes. Yes, people do find it rather annoying sometimes but it saves time.' Daniel leant back, his chuckle genuinely good-natured. He liked the idea of saving time.

Then she said coldly, 'I don't believe you.'

'What?'

'You heard.' She was calm and matter-of-fact. 'You like playing the field. You're not ready for anything that involves commitment.'

Daniel flinched. That word.

'See?' She pointed at his face and took a sip of water. Forty-love.

Vincenzo appeared with a bottle of Sancerre, and showed the label to Daniel, who managed a 'fine' to Vincenzo while thinking of his next move, if there could be

66

one. A waiter placed the asparagus in front of the two of them. Katie began her next attack. 'So you're a lecturer in body language?' Daniel was pleased she knew a bit about him, and nodded modestly as he picked up his wineglass to taste the Sancerre. He put it to his lips demurely.

'Bullshit psychology,' she jibed. He took an enormous swig of the wine, a murderous glint flashing across his eyes, which he tried to disguise by throwing his head back, so he could take a good look at the ceiling. He put the glass down and nodded, with an approving 'mmm' towards Vincenzo, unable to say anything more as his mouth was still full of a swig's worth of Sancerre, but he was fuming at her cheek. Vincenzo, used to seeing Daniel in control, smiled inwardly. Daniel seemed to have met his match.

Vincenzo poured. As he did, Daniel's eyes jumped between her glass, his glass and the bottle, as he debated whether to run out, kick her or call her a stuck-up cow. He waited for Vincenzo to leave, before leaning right over at her and saying cattily, 'I find it useful.' She looked dubiously, as he continued, 'It helps us to understand how our body language affects people's –'

'– Perceptions of us. I know. It's rubbish.'

'It is not rubbish. Are you going to do this all –'

'Yes.'

'Yes what?'

'What yes what?'

Then Daniel remembered the end of his sentence. And the beginning.

'Are you going to do this –'

'All evening?' she asked, and answered herself, 'Yes. I can't help it. Anyway, you don't strike me as a man who likes to waste time with unnecessary conversation,' and gave a big smile.

Daniel leant back, unsure what this meant – was it a come-on? This 'not wasting time' thing again. He smiled slowly, and gave her his sexy eyes, 'So . . .'

'So . . . ' said Katie, leaning back like Daniel.

'Well.' Daniel wasn't sure what to do. It could go either way – a snog or a punch, he wasn't sure yet.

But Katie stepped up a gear, her voice becoming almost threatening. 'Come on. Charm me. Win me over. I want to feel what it's like to fall under your spell.'

Her irony left Daniel all at sea, but he had to keep a tough, cool exterior, 'There's no spell. When two people meet like we did, do you know what it is? It's –'

'It's fate. Sorry, do go on.' She was enjoying herself.

Daniel was desperate. He'd try his last resort, 'Don't you think that making love is overrated? There's so much more to a healthy relationship.' He leant back with a wry grunt as Katie chewed her asparagus. He continued, 'Not that it shouldn't be mind-blowing.'

Daniel began to feel this tack would work. 'Sex . . .' he paused, but Katie was rather disinterestedly taking a sip of water, and toying with her asparagus. He carried on, only slightly daunted, '. . . is one of the only times in life when we give up power, control –'

'– And resort to basic human instinct,' they both said in unison.

She'd done it again! Finished his sentence! And with exactly the words he was going to use! It was infuriating. He exploded. For real.

'Jesus! What is it with you?' he hissed.

'What?'

'You're acting like a child . . . like . . . an immature . . . teenager . . . like a . . . ' He didn't say it.

She did. 'I am NOT A TIGHT-ARSED VIRGIN!' she yelled. He had been thinking this, as it might explain her odd behaviour, but he didn't particularly want to share his thoughts with the entire restaurant.

Some heads turned, and the restaurant fell silent. Katie got up, and screamed at him, 'And I do not look beautiful when I'm angry.'

Katie started to walk out. Daniel paused and then ran after her, passing Vincenzo, who was concerned that the asparagus hadn't been up to scratch.

Daniel was angry and bemused. How had she known exactly what he was going to say? Every time? And she'd chosen the oysters and asparagus. She kept interrupting him, saying what he was about to say, barely after he'd thought it. Could she read his mind?

She was going at quite a pace, and Daniel lagged behind her outside, as she strode across the cobblestone court-yard. 'Katie, I'm sorry,' he shouted. She walked on, her arms resolutely crossed.

'Katie, please. Look . . . I'm sorry.' He got just in front of her. She stopped, and glared at him, then at the river. He looked at it too. A duck quacked. She looked at her feet, then away from Daniel. There was a boat nearby. Nothing too grand, a pleasure boat for daytrips, but it could probably sleep four uncomfortably. Glistening white. He walked down some steps to it, and suddenly had an idea. He turned and asked, 'Whaddayou think?' while deliberately thinking, 'This is my boat. I own it.'

She trotted down the steps to take a closer look at the boat, and breathlessly enquired, 'How long have you had her?'

'Had what?'

'The boat.'

'Oh, the boat . . .' He looked at it. The duck kept quacking. 'I don't own a boat.'

'Wait, you just —'

'Caught you out. I never *said* anything.'

He had to find out. Could she read his thoughts? But she hadn't read them when he was lying about the boat. Was it that he hadn't been near enough? Or not looking at her.

He stared straight into her eyes.

'You can, can't you?' Read my thoughts, he thought. You can read my thoughts, can't you?

'No, you're wrong.' She returned his stare, but her voice had lost the assurance it had had inside. Her hands were pleading.

'I don't think so.' He sidled away, convinced he was right. Advantage Becker.

Chapter Five

How else had she known what he was going to say? And the exact words. She could read his thoughts. That would explain all the punches. Heaven knew what he must have been thinking when doing up his shoelace, and when he'd asked her out for dinner after she'd spilt his notes, and at Discretion. Heaven knew and so did she. All his thoughts, which were properly his, to hide and enjoy, but never let see the light of day, could be read by her. But not if he was far away, or not looking at her, the boat incident showed that. This was amazing. But scary.

He went towards the restaurant. She followed. Her petulance and anger subsided and she seemed relieved. She was. She told few people, and had been on edge tonight, undecided whether to tell Daniel or not. Her indecision had led her to taunt him, to will him to find out for himself, or be scared off by her weirdness. She didn't know how he'd take it. He waited for her in the courtyard. She caught him up, and they scurried back to Angelino's, where Vincenzo had cleared their asparagus, but not the Sancerre yet. He greeted their return with a smile. He'd cancelled the oysters.

Daniel told him they still wanted them. Katie ate hers, but Daniel's mind was buzzing with questions about her form of ESP. Surely this was fantastic? To read people's thoughts! What couldn't you do with that? He was all for going to a casino there and then. You could win thousands at poker with her!

71

Katie tried to calm him down, seeing that he wasn't just thinking about casinos and poker but letting his mind wander to how he could cope with the thing which he had earlier thought they might 'save time' before getting to.

He wanted to know all about it. What were the limits? Arm's length, she said, roughly, and the further away the more she had to concentrate. Looking them in the eye, close to, was the best. Her power was reduced when she was tired or drunk, and she hadn't yet come across anyone who could do it back to her, apart from her mother. No, it didn't work with animals, or with people on television. She tried to tell him it wasn't a wonderful party piece, but a curse.

'A curse?' he squealed, incredulously.

'That's right. A curse.' She began to regret letting him in on it. He might want her to do all sorts of tricks for him. She wasn't going to a casino.

'But why? It sounds like an endless source of fun. Like having a pair of X-ray glasses.'

Yes, thought Katie, but remember what happened to the man with X-ray eyes? He pulled them out in the end. Poor Ray Milland. But of course Daniel didn't know she was thinking that. He was too carried away by his own thoughts.

'Reading people's minds,' he enthused. 'Being able to see past what they want you to see. Wow.'

The waiter approached with the desert menu. They looked up at him. Daniel took charge, 'Oh, um, fresh fruit.' Katie stared after the waiter. Daniel was excited, mulling over the possibilities . . . Just think if she went on *Mastermind*! Or she could hire herself out to the police, at great expense, as a human lie detector.

'Oral sex,' hissed Katie.

'Sorry?' He gulped. She wasn't wasting time.

'Oral sex . . . the waiter. Just a moment ago.'

Daniel wondered if he'd missed something. Ah, that's what had been on the waiter's mind. She'd read it. He tried to say this, but it came out as, 'You, err . . . ' as he pointed at the departing waiter.

'Men's minds are sewers,' sneered Katie.

Daniel got up, ready for a fight. 'Right, I'm going to have a word.' How dare the waiter have lewd thoughts about his date! That was Daniel's privilege.

But Katie stopped him, 'And say what exactly?' Good point. Daniel's bottom found his seat again. 'Forget it. It happens all the time. You get used to it.'

The waiter brought the trolley of fresh fruit over. Katie chose the figs. Daniel gave the waiter a hard stare. The waiter cut the figs up, his eyes and lips deep in concentration as he cut the fig open to reveal the red flesh. Daniel looked on, fearing the worst, hopeful that the waiter wasn't thinking what he shouldn't. He was. Katie averted her gaze. But then she looked over at the waiter, her eyes exploded with anger, and she pushed his face down hard into the trolley. He recoiled and dropped to the floor. Katie was out of her seat and on her way to the door before Daniel could take it in.

She pushed past Vincenzo, as Daniel trotted behind. Vincenzo stopped him, years of politeness and respect for Daniel's past and future custom severely strained by the fact that his guest had just walloped one of his best waiters. The son of a good friend, whom he had promised he would look after and train, now lay prostrate by table five with fig juice all over his face. '*Scusa, scusa,*' he restrained the bewildered Daniel. 'Is something wrong, Signor Becker?'

'Yes,' affirmed Daniel, trying to summon righteous anger, whilst aware of the tenuousness of his complaint, and that Katie was getting away. 'Your waiter was having lewd thoughts about my companion.' As if to emphasise the point, and give himself strength, he strenuously pointed at himself on 'my companion'. Vincenzo was distraught. Paolo seemed such a nice boy. Okay, he may not know yet how to serve a veal escalope and sauce using only one move with the spoon and fork, but he didn't go round propositioning female diners.

'What? He told you this?' asked Vincenzo, mentally preparing the telephone call he would have to make to Naples before sending Paolo home.

Ah, thought Daniel. He'd hoped to avoid discussion of any details of the offence. 'No . . . he . . . err, well . . . he err.' He had to get out, so he took a deep breath, looked Vincenzo right in the eye, and announced triumphantly, 'He thought it,' and nodded conclusively, though he stopped himself just short of saying, 'And I thought this was a respectable establishment,' before striding boldly out.

Vincenzo was left bewildered, muttering, 'He thought it?' He looked at Paolo on the floor, slowly coming to, another diner trying to bring him round by wafting a mackerel under his nose.

Katie emerged from the restaurant. She had to get away from Daniel. He'd be livid with her. He came running out after her. Without looking back she shouted, 'Like sewers. I told you it was a curse.' She headed off to the left, then stopped. That way lay only a wall. She turned the other way.

Daniel, who'd been just behind her, was now in front of her, forced to walk backwards. 'I'll give you a lift.'

'No!' She wanted nothing from him. Just to go home.

Daniel, trotting backwards and out of breath, had no time to think of his body language. He had to see her again. 'Maybe we should go out again some time.'

Katie said nothing, she just headed off in another direction, leaving Daniel trailing.

'To a film. Or the theatre,' he flailed. Her silence forced him to keep talking. He bobbed about in front of her. 'Or whatever. Obviously, not soon – necessarily. But whatever.' She got past him. He laid a hand on her, 'Or a concert.' She stopped and looked at him. There was excitement in her eyes. And fear. He took her in his arms. She didn't resist. He gently moved his lips to hers. Closer and closer. But she spoke.

'We hardly know each other.' Daniel, pulling her a little closer, said nothing. She pulled away. 'What do you mean "so"? It matters to me.' There was anger in her voice, 'I want to be liked for my mind, not my body. There's more to life than lust: intellectual pursuits, the search for genius – My perfume? What about it? – The striving for knowledge – Great teeth? – To work out why we're here. If that's all you can think about you may as well say goodbye here and now.'

She headed off to a cab waiting nearby. Daniel stood his ground. That moment when their lips had approached would keep him going a long time. It had been genuine.

'Good looks and charm aren't what every woman looks for,' she shouted back at him. She got in the cab. It circled Daniel and headed out of the courtyard. She was slightly disappointed that he didn't run after the cab, but he was pleased with his resolve in not doing so.

He wandered back to the river and looked at it, listening to the duck quacking, pondering the night's events. A girl-friend with ESP who punches strangers. This was dangerous territory. But he couldn't stop now. Her beauty, her intelligence, her belligerence, hiding great charm, attracted him enormously. He went and asked the valet to retrieve his car. He considered going back in to apologise to Vincenzo, but realised his explanation of Katie's behaviour was rather unsatisfactory, and he'd better wait for another occasion.

He drove home, elated by the forthcoming challenge of winning Katie. She must like him, he thought, to have come to dinner in the first place, even if it was to bait him at first. But when he'd discovered her secret he'd detected relief on her part. The next few days would prove interesting. His dreams that night involved Katie and the boat. They were speeding along the River Thames, when Paolo the waiter emerged from below deck, carrying Harry's notes, only to be pushed overboard by a livid Katie. Shouts from a nearby cruiser, full of scientists in tweeds and corduroys, alerted Daniel and a chase began. Ahead of them, he spotted Harry, in a pedalo, pedalling furiously. And then he noticed Mrs Gonzalez, his cleaning lady, on the stern of his boat, with a rocket launcher, firing delphiniums into the air.

The next morning he dressed quickly, eager to tell Harry last night's news. He zipped along to work, not stopping to have his windscreen washed, but giving the girl an 'another time' shrug. This time the stairs weren't full, so he ran up them and along the corridor to Harry's office, where Harry was sitting cross-legged on his desk, chucking rolled-up pieces of paper into a distant wastebin.

'Harry – she came. She was early. And she's got ESP.'

Harry jumped to his feet, 'Woah, woah. She was there?'

'Yes. She arrived before me. Dressed to kill. And she nearly did kill a waiter.'

'Really?'

'Yes, she can't help it, you see. He was thinking about having oral sex with her, so she shoved his face in the figs.'

'Daniel – would you like some time in the Therapy Room?'

'No! I'm serious. That's why she punched me. She could read my thoughts. She can read everyone's thoughts. But only if they're fairly close.'

'Daniel, did she tell you this?'

'She confirmed it. But I'd worked it out. Harry, she's got ESP. It's amazing.'

'I don't believe you,' said Harry as he began shredding paintings.

Daniel took out his mobile phone, 'I swear.' He was truly smitten, he'd realised that this morning. And with a girl who could read his mind. Who could read his mind, and yet had still come on a date with him, and very nearly kissed him. He'd replayed the scene over and over again in his mind.

Of course, she'd started off being rude, and then had resisted the kiss, but her eyes and those moments as he'd held her told him that she couldn't fight her feelings for ever. Her very resistance was classic courtship display. He was ebullient, and had to share it with Harry. Though Harry pretended to treat Daniel's relationships as those of a hyperactive teenager, and often shrugged an 'oh no, here we go again' shrug as Daniel blurted out his latest folly, he loved it. He took great vicarious pleasure in it, in the same way he could enjoy his daughter Clare tucking into burger and ice cream, knowing that later, at home, Caroline would have proper food waiting for him.

Daniel finished dialling. 'Hallo, Joe? Oh, tell him Daniel Becker phoned. I want a delivery. To Katie Burrill. Natural History Museum. Just tell him The Usual. Don't worry. He'll know what it means.' Harry knew what it meant. He'd often thought that Daniel should have bought a share of Joe's Florist, it would have been cheaper, so enormous was the amount he'd spent over the years on conciliatory

bouquets, hopeful bouquets, see-how-the-land-lies bouquets, remember-me bouquets, consoling bouquets,
last-night-was-very-special bouquets.

This time, thought Harry, Daniel has gone potty. 'ESP?'
he said as Daniel pressed the End button on his mobile
phone. Harry collected the shreds while Daniel did his best
to convince him.

'It's the weirdest thing. I'd think something and she'd
know what it was – word for word.'

'Aha,' nodded Harry in mock agreement. He knew
exactly the sort of thing Daniel would have said – clichés,
and the obvious old, 'I just broke up with someone: she
didn't understand the real me.' He could have gone instead
of Daniel and said it for him.

'That's because you're transparent. My five-year-old
daughter can see through you. Women are like that.'

'No! This is different. She wouldn't let me finish –'

'– My sentences,' interrupted Harry, pleased to make his
point. 'See? Anyone can do it. She is having you on.'

Katie was not having him on. She'd first realised her talent
was something special when she was about Clare's age.
She'd noticed before, of course, but didn't kow that other
people couldn't read minds. She mentioned it to her
mother. Her mother looked hard at her, 'Yes, you've got it
too.' There was a note of disappointment in her voice.
'You mustn't tell anyone else. It's a very special gift, which
no-one else has.'

'Do you have it?' asked little Katie.

'Yes,' replied her mother, 'but it's a secret. Not even
your father knows.'

Katie had followed this advice very carefully. At no
point had she ever really considered it an advantage. She'd
never known what it was like not to have the ability to

78

read minds – she just couldn't imagine it – but she gradually began to realise that people's thoughts were not meant to be read, and were better staying in their minds. This was why she described it to Daniel as a curse. Nevertheless, it didn't stop her reacting to some particularly disagreeable thoughts that others might have about her.

This had somewhat curtailed her teenage love life. She soon got a reputation, thoroughly deserved, for being very frosty. She grew up in Somerset, in the idyllic little town of Wedmore, near the Cheddar Gorge and the Mendip Hills and was educated at the Ladies' College in Cheltenham. There were many pubescent boys in Wedmore and Cheltenham who got more than they bargained for at discos when asking her if she'd like to join them for the Slow One, invariably 'I'm Not in Love' by 10CC.

At Edinburgh University, she did meet a man whom she could trust. Gordon was studying linguistics and artificial intelligence. He had been the love of her life, or so she'd thought. He was a couple of years older than her. He liked expensive red wine; she didn't. He liked skiing; she didn't. He liked eating late; she didn't. She liked the country; he liked the city. He liked sleeping late; she didn't. He liked *Blind Date*; she didn't. It seemed a perfect match.

They both went on to postgraduate work, and lived together in a beautiful flat in Edinburgh's New Town, which was, of course, very old, with stone floors, high ceilings, spacious hallways, with large sash windows, through which could be seen rows and crescents of other Regency town houses.

She never told him her secret, which was a struggle, as she sometimes reacted in ways he couldn't understand because she had read his thoughts. But he loved her, and tried to take it all in his stride, and had proposed marriage. She'd known he was going to ask. It was during the Festival. They went to see an obscure German piece translated into Geordie couplets, and sat behind a man who looked a bit like Carlos the Jackal, who'd fallen asleep when Stefan, the hero, went out to buy a packet of tabs. Afterwards he took her to the Café Royal Oyster Bar in Edinburgh, bought champagne, and presented her with a ring. She'd said yes, delighted by his commitment, but worried about how they could live a life while he still didn't know her secret.

Her mother was delighted by the news, but went white with horror when Katie said she might tell Gordon. Katie's father had never known, and it was better that way. So Katie didn't tell him. The wedding was set for a year afterwards, during which time Katie got a research post at Imperial College, London. Gordon stayed in Edinburgh, finishing his PhD on dysfunctional speech, on the role of umms and errs, pauses and repetitions in conversation. To finance himself he took a research assignment with an American telephone company, who were trying to develop voice-activated machinery. Gordon's job was to log the varying pitches, tones, emphases and errors in recordings of the same sentence by different voices, covering all nationalities and all dialects. The sentence was "I would have preferred Aunt Monica to have visited in February", and after listening to it thousands upon thousands of times, Gordon would gladly have killed Aunt Monica, whatever month she decided to show.

They hadn't seen each other for six weeks when Katie visited, four months before the wedding. They were walking along the harbour front in Leith, the old port of Edinburgh, now a hive of yuppie flats and brasseries, when she suddenly told him. She could no longer bear it. Their life together could not go forward while she kept such a secret.

He stared at her.

'You don't believe me,' she said, 'but it's true. I'm doing it now.' His face melted in horror and confusion. 'Why didn't I tell you before?' she read his mind. 'Why did I tell you now? . . . Yes, all the time . . . I tried not to . . . and yes, it would explain all those times I was "funny" . . . mostly . . .'

He turned away from her, and the rest of their weekend together was spent in ghastly silence with the occasional muttering. Gordon felt it such a betrayal that their subsequent conversations on the telephone became more and more perfunctory and eventually she got a letter saying that it was all off. He felt he couldn't trust her. Her mother tried hard not to say, 'I told you so,' and didn't in so many words – just in many ways without using those words.

Since then she had determined to tell anyone to whom she was getting really close, and if they couldn't face it, better that they leave earlier than later. However, as yet nobody had come into that category. She threw herself into her work, travelling to archaeological sites, attending conferences, writing in journals, and rose up the ladder in her field. Once, when she was attending a conference in Glasgow, Gordon found her in her hotel lobby. This time it was she who couldn't talk, merely wishing him well, and saying she had to dash – to a café round the corner for the next two hours till she was sure he'd gone.

After she got home from Angelino's, she sat with a cup of peppermint tea for an hour, wondering about Daniel. Would it work? Did she want it to work? Should she have told him? She didn't really tell him, he'd guessed it. But she'd almost wilfully made him deduce it, she could see that. She couldn't work out why she felt attracted to him. He wasn't her type, he was far too shallow, certainly not an intellectual. And why had he gone for her? Surely he wanted some blonde with legs and tight clothes? What could they possibly have in common? If, as Mrs Dwyer often pointed out, it took eggs and flour to make a cake, who was the flour and who the eggs? And did they really want to be beaten together and baked? She wasn't sure. Her ESP didn't go as far as foretelling the future. But she wouldn't have wanted that. Life would be intolerable – you might never do anything. It was bad enough knowing what other people were thinking.

She sat on the tube the next morning, rather groggy after a poor night's sleep, worrying, and turning it all over in her mind. She tried not to look at her fellow passengers, so as to avoid their thoughts invading her own, but she couldn't avoid the occasional glance. Opposite were a middle-aged couple, holding hands, very much in love. The woman stroked the man's hair, which was receding a little. 'He's definitely losing his hair,' she was thinking.

Katie looked at the man, whose face gave no clue to his thoughts, which were, 'We're going to crash. I know it. Any second . . . now . . . Now!'

Katie looked at the woman and her thoughts. 'Maybe he'll look like Yul Brynner . . .' but all the man was thinking was, 'We'll crash! Any second . . . now . . . now.' It was tiring enough thinking her own thoughts; others' were exhausting, so Katie looked away. She looked up as a man came along the carriage, looking for a seat.

'I've got a gun in my pocket. I've got a gun in my pocket,' he was thinking. It was Parris. Katie was somewhat alarmed. He didn't look like he had a gun in his pocket, much less that he would know how to use it if he did. He had an anorak on over his jacket, and was searching determinedly for a seat. He would sit in a free one, come what may. None of the old 'oh no you have it' Parris, he would take any seat there was and grab it with both buttocks. He sat next to Katie. She looked at him again, trying not to be too obvious.

'I've got a gun in my pocket. I've got a gun in my pocket.' It seemed to be on a loop in his mind. He sat, and let out a sigh of pleasure. She moved one seat along. He looked at her and blinked. Why had she moved, he wondered? Perhaps she couldn't handle his chutzpah, perhaps the heat from the sexual vibes he was giving off were too much for her. Certainly Julie hadn't been quite sure how to handle them last night. She'd been peeling the potatoes for the cottage pie, and he'd sidled up behind her, grabbed her and demanded to have her on the kitchen table. In the ensuing mêlée, the sprouts had gone all over the place, and his glasses had landed in the mince. They'd ended up having take-away and watching Poirot in silence.

Now Katie was opposite a young woman, reading a copy of *Ulysses*, a book which Katie had bought as an undergraduate, convinced she would read it over the summer holiday and return armed and prepared for any late-night student discussion. Sadly, she'd never got round to it, and the yellowing receipt inside, which she'd kept as a possible bookmark, still lay inside the front cover, a monument to her failure. Next to the young woman sat a young black man who was reading *Ninety Minutes*, the football magazine, and was thinking, 'Why does everyone look so miserable on the tube?' The young woman looked up from her *Ulysses*, clearly unable to concentrate, as her thought was, 'God, I feel horny.'

The middle-aged couple were still hand in hand, but their thoughts were far apart, the man still thinking about an imminent crash, and the woman about what parts of the body, apart from Yul Brynner's head, her husband might appropriate, 'Kevin Costner's bottom and Al Pacino's eyes. Al Pacino's bottom and Kevin Costner's eyes. Kevin Costner's bottom and Al Pacino's eyes.'

Katie grinned, and glanced at the young woman, who was now staring at her, and thinking, 'Could make more of herself. Desperate for sex.'

Katie looked away sharply, catching sight of the young man, who thought everyone looked so miserable. He was thinking, 'Maybe if I smile, it might catch on. It might prove infectious. I might change the world.' Katie was delighted by this, and she smiled at him. He looked at her and thought, 'Psychopath.'

Katie got out of her seat in high dudgeon and got off, even though it was three stops too early. She strode down the platform, eager not to be spotted changing seats. Two-and-a-half carriages seemed far enough away from her former travelling companions, and she squeezed in as the doors shut.

Parris was still thinking about the gun in his pocket. And the lost cottage pie.

Katie found herself sitting again opposite Nigel Johnson, the young banking assistant. Delighted by *Cosmo*, and now on his way to a training course on 'PEPS – The Way Forward?', he had bought *Mademoiselle*, attracted by the promise of articles on 'Naturism Revealed', 'S & M in Surrey', 'Ten Ways to Stop your Fella Getting Bored', and 'Computer Sex – The Way Forward?'

Soon it was her stop – South Kensington – and she got off. Katie walked along the Cromwell Road to the Natural History Museum, wondering if Daniel might call her. She'd told him where she worked, and he had insisted on giving her his mobile telephone number and address. But she wasn't going to call him. Oh no, let him use all his charm on her. She wearily put her briefcase on her desk and donned her lab coat. Some samples had arrived from India by special messenger, and she was intrigued to see how they compared with samples from a previous find.

She was still staring at them intently through the microscope an hour later when there was a knock at the door. She didn't look up, and idly said, 'Yes?' Joe, the florist, with his white hair and beard, wearing a grey suit, stood in her office bearing a bouquet of champagne roses.

'Miss Burrill?' he asked, totally aware that it was her lab, since it said so on the door outside, but wanting to see her reaction of surprise and pleasure on seeing her floral tribute. Despite fifty years in the business of horticultural romance, he still got a thrill from that moment when the recipient first saw their gift.

Katie was not to be disturbed. Her eyes were glued to the microscope as she muttered, 'I'm busy.'

Joe put the flowers on the bench and left. But he'd be back, The Usual would require many trips. It was a long journey back to his van; down the stairs, and through the magnificent hall of the ancient museum, which housed a huge dinosaur skeleton, so it was ten minutes before he returned. He knocked again. This time she did look up. This time he had two bouquets of champagne roses. She got up from her microscope and asked who'd sent them. Joe looked at her and handed her a card.

'To my beautiful princess for a wonderful night from her wonderful knight'. This was The Usual message. She giggled, and was about to thank Joe, when she realised he'd gone. Oh well, she shrugged, and searched through her briefcase, trying to find the Angelino's card on which Daniel had written his number.

Daniel was in the seminar room, as a new 'set' – a cocktail bar – was being built for today's role-play situation. He was looking at his watch, toying with a maraschino cherry, expecting the delivery to be taking place about now and the phone call pretty soon after. Nobody could resist The Usual. He let it ring three times, before popping the cherry in his mouth and, answering. 'Daniel Becker, bull-shit psychologist, at your service.'

'They're beautiful,' said Katie.

'I'm glad you like them.'

Then Joe returned.

'Oh my God,' cried Katie as he came in with two more bouquets. She smiled and pointed out the remaining space on the bench to him.

'Can you tell what I'm thinking?' asked Daniel.

'Not over the phone.'

'Good.' Things were going very well for him: the Ice Maiden was beginning to thaw. He took the cherry out of his mouth. 'Can I see you tonight?' he ventured.

She played with her pencil. Yes, she was attracted to him. Yes, these flowers were lovely. Special. Maybe he wasn't just interested in playing the field any more. He really seemed to care. But if he did, he could wait. After a bad night's sleep, she didn't want to go out.

'No.'

'Oh,' said Daniel pausing deliberately. Fair enough, two nights on the trot might make her seem too keen. 'OK.'

'Well, maybe,' she said and quickly put the phone down. Daniel grinned to himself and ate the cherry.

Joe was far from finished. The Usual would take about forty minutes, and he made journey after journey through the great hall, nodding each time to the porter, who returned the compliment, and then up the stairs. Katie couldn't get back to work as she had to find somewhere to put all these roses. She had one vase that had been left there by the previous occupant. She had to search round for jugs, or anything, to contain the botanical invasion, and when Joe returned for the fifth time (she presumed it was Joe, as he couldn't be seen through the mountain of roses he carried) she was almost irritated.

'Look, this is getting ridiculous. Tell Mr Becker it's enough.'

Joe couldn't countermand Mr Becker. He couldn't leave here until The Usual had been despatched in its entirety. Joe tried to protest, 'But he ordered –' then decided to keep his mouth shut.

Katie looked at him suspiciously, and a couple of the roses in his hands began to quiver. 'He ordered what?' She stared deep into his eyes. And she knew what Daniel had ordered.

A couple of hours later, and the cocktail bar set had been erected and was in use. The lights were dimmed and music was blaring, just like a real bar. Bob Narley was serving, and various businessmen (including Norman Waddle and Something in Oil) were using assertiveness techniques to attract his attention. Parris was failing to get it. He bobbed up and down, waved his fingers, raised his eyebrows. Zero success. Daniel was watching carefully. He'd never yet given anyone their money back for his course, but he was wondering about making an exception for Parris.

'Parris,' he shouted from the back. Parris looked over, hoping to be let off, or for Narley to be told off for not playing the game properly. 'Remember the gun,' said Daniel.

Parris nodded. Yes, of course, the gun. So, with renewed determination, thrusting his hand into his pocket to grasp an imaginary gun, Parris fixed his eyes on the barman.

'Oi, you!' he yelled.

Narley was happily pouring out a bottle of lager from some Third World country with a repressive regime; the more repressive the regime, the more admired the lager in the wine bars of trendy London.

'Yes, *you*, dickhead.'

Narley finished pouring and put down the glass and bottle hard on the bar before advancing on Parris, who glared at him and said, 'I'm looking for service.'

Narley glowered back.

Daniel interrupted with, 'OK, everyone, back to your seats,' and a clap of the hands.

The music stopped and the lights came back on. Narley was right up close to Parris, and enquired, 'Who are you calling a dickhead?'

'You,' ejaculated Parris, aware of his gun and nothing else.

The other men went back to their seats, as Daniel tried to contain the situation, 'OK, game's over. Settle down.'

Slowly and deliberately, Parris said, through clenched teeth, 'I – want – a – drink,' staring at Narley's shoulder, giving him the same stare as when he was handing the figures over before, but now exponentially increased.

'Back to your seat, Parris,' ordered Daniel, now thinking that, far from giving him his money back, he'd have to ask for more money for time wasted.

'I want a drink,' he repeated plaintively to Daniel.

'All right, Parris. Take your hand out of your pocket and get back to your seat.'

Parris looked down. He took his hand out, but left the imaginary gun there, and looked at Narley, now smirking the smirk of the vindicated, and then at Daniel. With a flourish, he strode off, picked up his briefcase and anorak from his chair and walked out, content that he could learn no more here. As long as he had that gun in his pocket, he had all he needed. No-one had ever walked out of Daniel's class before; it was rather disconcerting, even if it was only Parris.

He was anxious to get back to his text, striding between the leather armchairs.

'A vast improvement! Well done, all of you . . .' He faltered a little as he saw the door closing behind Parris. Good riddance, he thought, but turned round and continued.

'Remember, life is –'

'– a game with set rules,' came the chorus from his class. Good, thought Daniel, now we're getting somewhere, but he was halted by a thought about Katie. She had said 'maybe' to him on the phone, about tonight. 'Maybe' meant 'yes', he was sure, so he'd call later, mid-evening. Eightish.

He meandered around the chair in which sat Something in Oil.

'Women . . . ' he muttered, letting it hang in the air, then continued. 'Women are suckers for the broader, more sensitive approach. They're particularly keen on a hint of weakness.' He picked out his glasses from an inside pocket and put them on. 'That means no guns. And, of course, they love to be flattered. They like to feel . . . special.' He let the last word ooze out, with more than a hint of Sacha Distel.

The door at the back of the room opened. 'Joe?' exclaimed Daniel. What was the florist doing here? He had brought a large wreath. Daniel went to him and took the wreath. 'From her?' he whispered.

Yes, nodded Joe, apologetically.

Daniel said loudly, 'Thank you, Joe,' as if Joe were a carefully trained assistant who had brought in this wreath right on cue, just as planned.

Daniel wandered back amongst his pupils and pronounced, 'With this wreath we lay to rest the weakness that held us back, that prevented us from fighting to dominate our surroundings and control our destiny. It shall not be mourned. Rest in Peace. Amen.'

'Amen,' repeated his class, obedient as ever.

Daniel dismissed them, 'OK, that's it for today,' and they swivelled off their chairs and headed out of the room, leaving Daniel all alone with his thoughts and the wreath. Why had she done this? This wasn't supposed to happen. The last thing she'd said was a 'maybe' meaning yes, he'd thought. Normally The Usual meant he had things perfectly under control. Frustrated, he threw the wreath in the air. His mind raced as it ascended. What was going on? Who was this woman who punched first, talked second, could read his mind, said an encouraging 'maybe', then sent a wreath? She was far from Usual. High up in the air went the wreath, like a frisbee, and Daniel watched it descend back towards him. He grabbed it just before it hit the ground, and muttered through gritted teeth, 'Control.'

Chapter Six

Daniel went to see Harry, who was quietly snoozing at his desk. 'I need some relaxation,' he snapped as he put down the wreath. Harry looked at the wreath. This was a little worrying.

'Is everything all right?'

'It will be,' replied Daniel, heading towards the darkened Therapy Room.

'No, you can't go in ther–' Too late. Daniel had opened the door, and let in a shaft of light which illuminated someone sitting in a smock, painting in the darkness.

It was Parris, like a frightened rabbit in a smock caught in headlights. After the initial shock, he gave a wan grin. 'What are you doing here?' demanded Daniel.

Harry pulled Daniel out and shut the door. 'What is he doing here?' repeated Daniel.

He clearly needed calming down, and Harry spoke softly, 'Look, it's no big deal. He just likes to come here for a few minutes . . . after one of your sessions.'

Daniel remained uncalmed, 'I've never taught such a –'

'– Junior librarian.' This took Daniel aback somewhat. Most of his pupils were in finance or major corporations. He found it difficult to imagine Parris coping in big business, or even small business. A librarian, eh?

'Really? I wondered.'

'Needs all the power he can get.' Harry looked at the wreath, 'Who's died?'

Daniel was still fuming. 'Not who. What. She sent it to me.'

'Aeah,' grunted Harry. No wonder he was so agitated.

'Joe must have said something,' continued Daniel.

'Doesn't sound like Joe.' No, Joe was most discreet. He had to be. It wouldn't do for Daniel's florist to go round blabbing: 'Oh, these aren't as big as the one for that brunette last week'; 'He'll expect at least a shag after these'; 'Just a bunch of chrysanths – you can't have been much good last night'; 'You should see where I'm going next for him, I've got a vanful of lilies.' Joe wouldn't have said anything.

It dawned on Daniel. Joe wouldn't have said anything. But he would have *thought* something. 'The Usual,' said Daniel, 'of course. She read his mind. I asked for the bloody Usual.' Daniel was mentally kicking himself for his crassness. He had to play by a whole different set of rules this time.

Harry could see that Daniel really believed it. Maybe she *had* read Joe's mind. Perhaps she could, after all. Let it ride. 'That would do it,' he said. 'So, what's your next tactic?'

'That's it. If she's going to be so immature, she can take a walk. I don't need the hassle.'

Harry wasn't fooled. He could see that Daniel would rise to the challenge. Besides, Harry had seen Katie. If he was in Daniel's shoes he wouldn't give her up lightly. Wrily he said to Daniel, 'You know, if you want someone to believe you, you should look them in the eye.'

How dare he! How could Harry possibly read his body language? Daniel wasn't going to go after her, whatever happened. She could ESP to her heart's delight as far as he was concerned. There was always Lucy, she didn't muck about reading your mind. She played tough but fair. And what might Discretion dating agency come up with? He'd been through the worst of it now, the initial trauma of going there, he could easily return and see what they had to offer.

'I swear to you, I have no intention of seeing her again. She's history.'

There was no convincing Harry. 'You don't want to see this girl again?'

'No!' Daniel was getting angry. How come all of a sudden Harry was so smug and knew everything? 'Look, why don't you believe me?'

'Well, it could have something to do with your arms.'

Daniel looked down. His arms were indeed begging Harry to believe him. OK, he accepted it. She had got to him. And after only one date. It was pitiful. One date and three punches. What was he going to do? One date, three punches and a hundred quid's worth of champagne roses. And she was calling the shots. Damn.

He drove home. Aggressively. Maybe he'd have a game of squash tonight. Or go to the gym. Or something that involved hitting something hard. 'Come on!' Some twerp in a Metro was dawdling in front of him. Honk! Honk! There was nothing coming the other way. Who cared if it was only a side street with cars parked on either side, he wasn't going to get stuck in a funeral cortège. 'Sunday driver!' So he overtook, and zoomed on.

Seconds later he saw a blue flashing light in his mirror. 'No way! There's just no way!' he screamed, but he pulled in. It was the cop. The same cop on her motorbike. Was she following him? Well, he'd done nothing wrong. Nothing at all. But there was mitigation. He leapt out of his car, shouting at the top of his voice, anger combining with a wish to be heard through the helmet she was wearing.

'No way. No fucking way! I mean, what is it with you? Why do you keep following me around? Do you fancy me or something?'

The cop took off the helmet. It was a man. It wasn't her. And the man was not amused, much less did he fancy Daniel. 'That's very interesting, sir. Would you like to follow me down to the station?'

'I'm very busy. My father ... he's in intensive care ... and my new baby boy ... he's in intensive care ... and my wife ... is prone to uncontrollable seizures.'

'Yes, sir. Just follow me, sir. We're facing the right way.'

When they got to the station the cop was still unimpressed by anything Daniel had to say. Daniel followed him, mouthing excuses, appealing to his better nature, even thinking of a bribe at one point but deciding against it. For the policeman it was water off a duck's back. Indeed, if Daniel had been trying to reason with a duck he might have had more success, such was the lack of response.

As they entered the police station, the duck waddled over to a desk, so Daniel tried someone else, behind a counter, not in motorcycle leathers, so possibly more senior. 'So they phoned me and obviously I jumped straight into the car, which is why I was speeding ... he's in intensive care.' Quack-quack ... oops, as Dave Lee Travis might have said. Daniel tried another officer. 'And ... I've been under a lot of pressure at work,' he protested with all the force of a child whose face is covered in chocolate but who denies all knowledge of the whereabouts of the Club biscuit.

Desperate, he now tried honesty, 'And my love life is in a state of absolute turmoil,' he shouted to no-one in particular. No-one in particular responded, so he sat down, and got down to the serious business of feeling sorry for himself.

A door opened and in came the female cop. A friendly face at last, and one that might listen to him, Daniel sprang to her.

'OK, what's going on?' she demanded, the tenderness of their previous meetings now evaporated. She'd read the arresting officer's notebook. He got up and tried a smile. She was having none of it.

'Look, I thought he was you,' he said ruefully.

She read from the notebook, 'No fucking way . . . D'you fancy me or something?'

Shit, thought Daniel, his face covered in metaphorical chocolate. She advanced towards him, forcing him back against the wall.

She was angry now, haughty even, 'No more lies. No more newborn babies. No dying fathers. OK? I'm on to you, Mr Becker.' She reached up and grabbed his lapels and concluded, 'No more bullshit.'

The professional control freak was way out of his depth. Shocked by her anger, he slipped back into a chair. Zero status. 'All right. OK,' he demurred quietly.

She smiled and told him to wait there. He sat, miserably contemplating his fate. A minor court case, points on his licence, bad publicity, he could just see the smirk on the face of Murray Henry, his breakfast TV enemy. And Harry's. No, wait. He could get a good lawyer, and the case would be dropped. Yes. He was Daniel Becker. He could get what he wanted. That was his profession.

A couple of minutes later the cop returned with two mugs of tea. 'Sorry it took a while, but this is better than the stuff from the machine.' He took it. It was so hot he could only sip it.

'Now, what's all this about your love life being in turmoil?' She ripped the pages out of the notebook, and placed them delicately on her lap. 'Honestly, this time.' She said it with such force, yet concern, that Daniel knew he should tell the truth. And she'd probably rip up those pages.

He told her about Lucy. The shoelace. The notes. The waistcoat. The dating agency. The date. The ESP. The waiter. The Usual. The wreath.

She listened intently, slowly grinding the pages into a ball. Daniel asked about her. A little reluctantly at first, she told him some details about herself. She'd married young, to her teenage sweetheart. Daniel couldn't imagine it. He'd changed so much since he was a teenager. Yes, so had she, she said, but marriage wasn't about standing still, it wasn't about 'growing together', whatever that meant, but it meant that two individuals could find their true selves, become more fulfilled than if they were not together, their being together actually enhancing their chances of being their true individual selves. This was deep stuff to hear from a traffic cop, and he needed the few moments' respite provided by her going to get a top-up of tea.

What should he do? He'd told Harry he wasn't going to see her again. Harry didn't believe him. But what sort of a future could he have with a woman who knew what he was going to say? Where was the mystery? He'd have to work hard on 'decoy thinking'. But imagine birthdays with her, as she unwrapped her presents . . . 'Oh yes, that, I remember when you thought of that . . . I thought you were going to get a blue one . . . £14.95, eh? You could have got the more expensive one.' Nightmare.

And sex. Yes, sex. If she knew what he was thinking . . .

Hang on, this might not be so bad. There were certain things better left unsaid, but if he *thought* them . . . she already thought men's minds were sewers, she couldn't be shocked. But what about for her? There were definitely things he might think about her that he wouldn't want her to know, things he couldn't help thinking, about her, or her body, or about silly things that pop into your mind just at the height of passion. Like: what was the name of the actor who played Private Sponge in *Dad's Army*? Did I pay my credit card bill? What was the first name of Mr McDermott, my chemistry teacher? Of course, you might *deliberately* think some of these things, especially if you're a man, in the height of passion. So where would that leave Katie? It must be terrible for her. So terrible, perhaps, that she was still a . . .

Hmmm. 'I am not a tight-arsed virgin.' Her words. No, wait, they were his words, he'd thought them, she'd said them. But had he really thought them? He couldn't remember. That was the trouble with thoughts, they popped in and out of your mind, often with scarcely enough time to catch them, some becoming articulated verbally, others wafting into the ether, safely, harmlessly. Until she came along.

What was he going to do? A mug of steaming hot tea landed in his hands. His friend the cop smiled down at him. 'You've got to go and tell her you're sorry.'

'What, in a couple of days, when she's realised how silly she was?'

'No, now. Be yourself and don't be a prat. Just go and say sorry, no tricks, just see what happens.'

She was right, of course. You couldn't fool Miss ESP. The Usual wouldn't wash with her.

'What do you mean you've never heard of castrate?' Miss ESP was playing with her computer Scrabble. 'I castrate, you castrate, we castrate,' she conjugated, as if to persuade the logophile machine. Around her were a couple of vases of champagne roses, which she'd brought home to relieve the congestion in her lab.

The man who had programmed the computer Scrabble had made a mistake. When putting in the words from the dictionary, he'd spilt his coffee at '**Castor** 1. Oily brown liquid obtained from glands of beaver and used in per-fumes. 2. Small wheel on swivel. 3. Horny external knob inside horse's leg', and lost his place while getting the J-cloth, left out 'Castrate', and gone straight on to 'Casual Accidental, unmethodical, careless'. A situation wrought with irony. He'd been too busy looking for the word 'slacks' in the definition of 'casual' (as in winter casuals) to notice his error.

It was not the first mistake he'd made. A typing error had meant that the machine now laboured under the mis-apprehension that the word 'Clunge' existed. A moment's lapse, brought about by the arrival of the birthday cake for Barry from computer backgammon, had let to 'Eclectic' being spelt with seventeen Cs. Ececcccccccccccclectic'.

'It's just a verb for God's sake,' complained Katie, but the machine was not going to let her have castrate. Little did she know that she could have got a double-word score and bagged herself fifty points if she'd used her C in Clunge, using the U already used in Lurk. Given an infinite amount of time, she might have come up with this, theoret-ically at least, but then so would the proverbial monkey, if he wasn't too knackered after writing all of Shakespeare's plays. But in the meantime, she was distracted by the chess machine beeping.

'A good move, if a bit obvious,' she said to the machine, fully aware of her comment's aqueousness vis-à-vis the computer's quack-quack-hood; it remained as unmoved as Daniel's arresting officer. She moved the computer's piece, then made her own move.

'Queen takes knight. Queen demolishes knight. Queen jumps up and down on knight.' She was enjoying herself, as Daniel Becker's grinning face stuck in her mind. Stupid man. The Usual. A posh dinner, a few smooth words, a ton of roses and he thought he was in. What a fool. Then she looked closely at the chess machine. Checkmate!

'My God, I think I've won!' She'd never won before, apart from that one time when the computer's knight had gone missing and she'd had to use a golf tee instead, but she was sure it had confused the poor thing. 'This calls for a celebration,' she declared, and headed straight for the fridge. She tenderly opened the door and pulled out a big Toblerone, the sort that you used only to be able to get in airport duty free shops till someone wised up and started selling them in supermarkets and petrol stations. They're so big that teeth alone can't do the job, you have to use your hands to break them into bite-sized portions.

Daniel was getting an escort from his traffic cop friend. She led him all the way to Katie's front door. He gingerly got out of his car. All the way there he'd been weighing up the pros and cons. And the cons were very heavy.

They pulled up, and as she took off her helmet, Daniel said, 'Maybe she needs a day or two, just to think things over.'

'Maybe I need a day or two to reconsider your driving offences.'

'She may tell me to piss off.'

'I wouldn't blame her if she did,' she retorted pondering on whether to preach to him on the necessity of having to face this eventuality, using as her text chapter five, verse six of the Cliché Bible, 'No pain, no gain'. She decided against it and continued, 'But I can't read your mind. Maybe she'll see something in there that I'm missing.'

Daniel headed up the steps to the front door.

She shouted after him, 'And remember, if at all possible, *think clean*,' before starting up her motorbike and heading off.

He was alone. He sighed and pressed the buzzer. What if she was out? He could run away! But her light was on.

Maybe she left it on to scare burglars away. Daniel had often wondered if burglars were fooled by such things. He knew one bloke who lived on a particularly tough estate in Stockwell, south London, who had been broken into so often that he left the lights *off* when he was *in* and *on* when he was *out*, just to fool them. But what if they'd have broken in when the lights were off? Would he have 'sorted' them? Or would they have 'sorted' him?

Daniel was about to press the buzzer again, ready to leave pretty soon after, when the door opened, and there was Katie, her mouth full. 'Wharrayouwant?' One of the few advantages of being a grown-up is the ability to get large amounts of chocolate into your mouth without getting it all over your face and hands, and once one has passed this threshold of knowledge it is difficult to understand how those on the other side cannot achieve this seemingly simple feat. Pick up the chocolate and put it in your mouth, using the conveniently placed conduit of the lips. Very straightforward. And yet any young child will, given free rein, almost instantaneously achieve a standard scatter pattern on the face, which if one didn't know, one would have thought had been carefully and painstakingly arranged by a top-flight special effects make-up designer. How do they manage to get chocolate into so many obscure places? And with such consistency? Why should so much end up on the cheek, in closer proximity to the ear than to the more profitable area of the lips? And the forehead? (Another advantage of adulthood is the opportunity to serve oneself with sprouts, thus being able to take and eat a smaller portion, instead of being served by another person allegedly better qualified in these things.)

Daniel was not immediately aware of the contents of Katie's mouth. Had he been, he might have asked, 'How on earth did you get an entire piece of Toblerone into your mouth? Have you no regard for your own dental engineering?' As it was, he said, 'I . . . what?'

Katie, anxious to make herself understood, swallowed the chocolate and repeated, 'What do you want?'

Now he was on the spot. He had to put it into words. No easy. 'Well . . . I . . . I . . . I wanted to, err . . . Why don't you read my mind?' Dammit, yes, why should he have to do all the work? She knew what he was thinking, probably better than he, why prolong the agony?

'I want to hear you say it.'

'OK.' He took a break. 'OK.' Another breath. A deep one. 'I'm sorry. That's all. I just wanted to say I'm sorry. If I seemed flippant. Or casual. (As in unconcerned, nonchalant, careless, not as in winter casuals. He felt no need to apologise for his garments/slacks/daywear.)

'Or insincere,' she added. This was very hard for Daniel. He wasn't used to apologising, unless it was part of a carefully planned strategy.

'Or insincere,' he repeated. Katie gave him a long hard look. He was genuinely contrite. He must be. He didn't know what to do next. Tactics were out the window. He turned to leave, but hesitated, half expecting her to say something. She didn't. So off he went to his car. She let him go down the steps. One, two, three.

'Where are you going?' she asked, making him turn back, looking to her for help, 'I thought you had something planned for this evening.'

Well, yes he did. Usually the second date was at this little place, just down the road from his place. Friendly, converted pub, newspapers with those wooden poles down the middle so you can't steal them, eccccccccccccclectic menu – ranging from cajun to stir-fry, with some Italian thing that Lucy had misread as 'tombola' first time round, and jazz on Fridays with improv comedy on Saturdays. And a late licence. Maybe back to his place afterwards.

'I did ... have something planned,' he confessed, 'But ... but what I was going to do was take you to all the places I've been before. And ... and well, I don't feel like doing that any more. Not with you. But I ... don't know where to start.' She smiled at him. Daniel 'How to Influence People' Becker was at a loss.

'Fine', she said. 'Let's go for a walk.'

She went to get a coat, while he waited outside. A walk? What did this mean? How could he keep the upper hand in this situation? Where would they go? What if they bumped into someone he knew? Someone whose thoughts she could read, who might be thinking something unwholesome, so would get hit, or was thinking something about Daniel that would get him hit? The possibilities were appalling. But what could he do? He just had to go with it.

She came out again, her mouth full of fresh chocolate, and proffered something, "Hereavthis.' It was a whole chunk of Toblerone. Daniel, attempting to be more demure than his companion, took a small bite, then another, as they walked along. She looked at him, questioningly. He nodded and shoved it all in. So the next few minutes passed with no conversation as they grappled with the chocolate. Katie wondered what future palaeontologists would make of their teeth. 'They seemed to have a liking for this substance which was known to have debilitating effects on the state of their teeth. And yet it also appeared to have ritualistic uses, as evidenced by the smears on the faces of the children of the tribe. Also, ice cream Mars Bars seemed very popular.'

They wended their way through the residential streets of Chalk Farm, and northwards towards Hampstead. Daniel decided not to try and hold her hand. Far too early. And she had her hands firmly planted in her coat pockets. They walked past the end of the evening rush-hour traffic, stationary and impatient.

He told her about himself; university, before that, school in Surrey, where his parents still lived, the first girl who broke his heart – she caught the same train as him, he couldn't remember which school she went to, but they had a blue uniform, and she went with a much older boy to the first disco he went to, and he had to console himself by skulking in the corner and trying to identify with 'I'm Not in Love' by 10CC. She wouldn't believe that this romantic underachievement had gone on long for him. No, he admitted, but he wanted to know more about her romantic history.

She described it as uneventful. She'd attempted one large mountain, rather than the numerous hills she assumed he'd climbed. She'd been hurt, yes, but had come out of it now. Daniel wanted to know his name, but she didn't tell him. For her, going to Mrs Dwyer was just a way of dabbling – she wasn't looking for another Big One, as her work was too important. Daniel nodded sagely, this was all fairly standard stuff. He wished he could read *her* thoughts. Was she frightened of him, of giving way to any feeling for him, or was she supremely confident?

They reached the edge of Hampstead Heath as night was falling. 'This way,' he said, confidently. 'No, this,' she said, just as firmly, pointing the other way. In the end, they went in a third direction, heading into the wilds. She seemed to be in charge, vaguely, as she said she came here quite regularly. Daniel was content to let her lead the way.

At one point, she stopped and looked at him. 'Why did Lucy leave you?'

He was a little taken aback, 'How did you . . .?'

'You were thinking about her, and that she never liked walking.'

'Yes.'

'Well?'

103

'I suppose she left because I made her. Maybe I didn't. Maybe she was going anyway – she certainly seemed better off once she had. But I think I hankered. Yes, I was hankering.'

'For what?' She looked at him, then away quickly.

'For a palaeontologist?' he attempted. They walked on.

They reached a crossroads. Katie stopped. She was lost. She looked at the various routes open to them. Daniel took her arm. She pulled away, and pointed one way out (Thesis). He pointed in the opposite direction (Antithesis). In the end, they went off in a third direction (Synthesis), such was the dialectic of their Route Planning. Hegel would have been proud, though it is not known whether he formulated his epistemology of opposing ideas leading to a higher truth through taking his girlfriend for a walk in the park and not knowing which route to take, or after a few bevvies at his local, the Dog and Zeitgeist. Indeed, had he been able to advise Berti Vogts before the 1994 World Cup, he could perhaps have resolved the contradictions between playing a flat back four or the sweeper system.

They reached a clearing. Stone steps led up the hillside, with trees on either side. They looked at each other. Without saying a word, they both started to run up the steps, racing one another. At the top, out of breath, they found themselves in a colonnade of twisting ivy. While Katie took it all in, Daniel darted behind a pillar without her seeing. She walked down the colonnade, shouting his name.

'Daniel . . . Daniel . . . Come on.' No reply. 'OK,' she said, as if she were above this game and could wait all night and he could jolly well stew wherever he was. Several metres behind her, Daniel appeared. She stood still and silent. He tiptoed toward her. She knew he was there, but didn't turn round, just smiled. Very gently, he progressed right up to her. She let him. Gradually, he moved his lips to her neck. She knew she must do something, and gently said, 'No. Not yet.'

He understood, and they carried on walking through the colonnades and over the Heath. They watched the dawn come up, both feeling confident and relaxed. Daniel was happy to let his regular agenda go out the window, and see what happened. He could afford to take his time. They wandered back to her flat, past the early morning rush-hour traffic, even some of the same cars, now facing the other way. They passed Belsize Park tube station, where Nigel Johnson was buying an early morning copy of *Bella* from the newsstand.

They reached her front door, and, though she could think of nothing but sleep, she knew what he was going to say, even before he'd thought it. 'Tonight. C'mon, let's meet tonight.'

She sighed and said, 'I'd like to, but –'

'– You want to.' Daniel was confident now, he knew she didn't spend the night with many men on the second date, even if they had both kept their clothes on. 'I know you do. If you like someone your pupils get bigger.'

She smiled, and finished her sentence. 'I'd like to, but I don't want to feel under any pressure. Anyway, I'm working today.'

Daniel was not giving up. 'I said tonight,' and with a sing-song voice told her, 'Your pupils are getting larger.'

'You're impossible!'

'They are huge!' He was enjoying himself.

There was no arguing with him so she pursed her lips, gave him a peck on the cheek and opened the front door. 'Great,' he said, 'I'll ring you later. Bye!' and scuttled down the steps to his car.

Chapter Seven

As he drove, he felt a growing sense of confidence. He'd spent the whole night with a woman, without getting horizontal. He was proud of himself, and excited. Surely when they did, wouldn't it be all the better for waiting? Yes. But how long would he have to wait? No, he shouldn't think like that. Wait for her to be ready. He needed time, too. But not much. One more date? Surely no more than three? No, it wasn't a question of arithmetic. It was a question of two mature people, her understanding the real him, and him understanding the real her.

She had a head start, though. She could read his thoughts. However, were his thoughts the real him? And which thoughts – the unconscious or the conscious? He vaguely remembered some philosophy (which he'd had to do as a subsidiary course for a year. It was either that or statistics, and probability had given him a headache in the third form at school when he'd been trying to think about that girl in the blue uniform) which held that conscious thoughts could be further broken down into 'enjoyment' and 'contemplation'. 'Enjoy' not in the sense of having a good time with, but, instead, to experience, and 'contemplate' as in thinking about it. So, if you see a chair, you 'enjoy' the act of seeing, and 'contemplate' the chair. Thus you would 'enjoy' a fearful thought while faced with a lion, and then later, after a cup of hot sweet tea and a brandy, you might 'contemplate' fear. He found this distinction interesting, but had also been intrigued by another, perhaps less intellectually rigorous theory, formulated by the college barman.

Put briefly, and in Latin, it was '*in vino veritas*', or 'it's difficult to lie when you're pissed'. All the horrible, stupid, irrational, childish things we say when drunk are what we think anyway, but usually the lack of alcohol prevents us spilling the beans. Perhaps we didn't even know we were having the thoughts, but sufficient intoxication provides illumination. Though appealing and straightforward, this theory was profoundly depressing. Could people's 'true' selves be so appalling? Covered with such a thin veneer of respectability? How drunk did you have to be to get to the true self – one hundred per cent? What was the coefficient of truth/drunkenness? Six pints equals fifty per cent?

And what could Katie 'read' in Daniel? What did she see? The sordid, pathetic, yet highly lyrical specimen he'd once become on that occasion when he'd gone to a Test Match (England versus Australia at Trent Bridge. Because it was raining, he had repaired to the bar, and for some unknown reason had begun drinking gin and tonic – a highly unusual choice for him – at eleven in the morning, having blotted out totally from his mind the danger stemming from the first ingredient)? Or the one who was caring and sensitive and vulnerable and generous? Or the confident, articulate, controlled lecturer he was during office hours? Or the one who couldn't stop thinking about getting her kit off?

He thought that perhaps all these could be his true self. Perhaps he had a multiple personality? He'd read about someone in Wyoming who had nine different personalities. That must have made shopping difficult, because, apparently, they all had different diets. One was vegetarian, one was vegan, one was on a macrobiotic diet, and one was a strict carnivore. He didn't know about the other five

– perhaps there was one who could only eat sprouts, another who only ate Toblerone, and another who was really weird and could only eat fettucine with mint jelly while watching a video of *Herbie the Love Bug*.

His mind was wandering, he knew. But what if Katie had been with him while he was having all these thoughts about thinking? Would she think he was mad? These were extreme circumstances, though – he hadn't had any sleep, and he was falling in love. Falling in love? Eeek. He tried not to think anything for a few moments. But he had to think about driving. Then the traffic cop popped into his mind. Thanks to her, he'd grasped the nettle, and it had worked out well. He should let her know the good news.

He came to a traffic light as it turned to red. He pulled up, then looked both ways, revving the car impatiently. Two cars were approaching from the right. He waited for the first to go by, then slammed his foot down and screeched through the red light, making the second swerve slightly. In an instant he saw in his mirror a familiar leather-clad figure on a motorbike. She came alongside him, and he gave her a thumbs-up sign. She lifted her left hand and gave an A–OK sign in return, and dropped back.

He drove on, heading for Harry's place in Camden. They weren't going to work today. One of Daniel's corporate clients had challenged him to a game of paintballing, involving men (and sometimes women) running around in the countryside and firing paint pellets at each other.

Harry was still having his breakfast, or more precisely, still supervising Clare having hers. Caroline was scathing about the day's activity. 'So you're going to run around playing at soldiers with other grown men?'

'It's a great way of relieving tension,' explained Daniel, 'and perhaps men need these sorts of things in modern times. Our male ancestors would have been in touch with their masculinity – they'd go hunting every day, risking their lives, to bring home the family's nourishment. Nowadays the only danger is having a dodgy wheel on a trolley at Tesco's.'

'And it's mostly women who hunt the food now.'

'Yes, and what does the poor man do? He goes and sits in an office, or stands at a machine all day. He needs to find the animal within himself.'

'Or the child,' added Caroline.

'Look, it's fun and we're going and that's that,' said Harry, getting up and taking Clare's last Marmite soldier with him.

'You could come too,' suggested Daniel to Caroline, unhelpfully.

'So, who's the opposition today?' asked Harry, once they were in the car and heading towards the M3.

It was a firm of investment bankers. 'McNeill, Alcock and Coton – always send me lots of their executives, and last year my team stuffed them at cricket, so this year they suggested this.' Daniel went on to describe who was going to be playing for his team: Nick Kenrick, the osteopath in the unit next to Harry's, a useful slow left-arm bowler who, if his darts was anything to go by, would be a demon marksman; Bill Denney, Daniel's accountant, who'd once had a trial for Crewe Alexandra, but now had a pot belly; Abdou, head waiter at his local Austrian restaurant, who was an unreconstructed Bennite; Philip, a videotape editor, whom Daniel had met when making the video of *How to Lose Friends and Influence People*, who was six foot four, and an obscenely fast bowler who had taken five wickets in last year's match.

Harry, who had made a promising eighteen in that match, even though he insisted on batting as if it were baseball, was heartened. This sounded like a useful squad.

He asked if Katie were coming. No, said Daniel, even though her ESP might have come in handy when searching for the enemy in thick foliage, but he thought it best not to plunge her into something like this so early in their relationship.

Harry read the blurb. Each player would be issued with paint pellets, a pump-action gun with which to shoot them, a camouflage jumpsuit, belt, team ID, and goggles. The point of the game was to capture the opposition's flag and get it back to your base. If you got marked by a paint pellet, you were out for that game, and had to go back to the Neutral Zone until the next game – which generally lasted for half an hour. Daniel wasn't too keen on this. He preferred the indoor laser game, where if you were hit, you lost Energy, but you had to be hit several times before your Energy was all gone and you had to go back and get recharged. Lucy had been remarkably good, her killer instinct being surpassed only by that of Nick Kenrick, the calming, soothing osteopath, who had so often and so sensitively manipulated Daniel's bones. Once armed with a laser gun he became a man possessed and had taken particular exception to a ten-year-old boy who had had the temerity to aim in his general direction, provoking Nick to blast him with four hundred megacharges.

They arrived at the site, somewhere in Hampshire. They were all there – Nick, Bill, Philip, Abdou. They'd been told to wear sturdy footwear; Bill had climbing boots and Philip had trainers. The opposition looked confident. Daniel recognised all but one of them. Big Dave, as he was introduced, had suspiciously apposite-looking footwear that was spattered with paint. A ringer, Daniel was sure. They were issued with their equipment, and briefed. Never take off the goggles, never shoot at anyone's face. The Adjudicator's word is final. Don't shoot at the Adjudicator. No kicking. Extra paint pellets available for extra money. No drinking. No litter. If you've been 'got', walk with your armband raised above your head. No shooting at someone with their armband raised above their head.

Then they had to sign a form, saying that they understood it was dangerous, that they'd abide by the rules, that they'd give back the equipment or pay a lot of money, and they or their heirs or executors wouldn't sue if anything, you know, went wrong. Or something like that, Daniel skimmed over it and signed. Their safety record was one hundred per cent, and he didn't intend to pinch the stuff.

Daniel's team – the Red team – was escorted to their start point by a man with a Welsh accent. A whistle blew and the game was on. Within fifteen minutes the other side had won the first game. Big Dave was, indeed, highly proficient. He not only knew how to fire the gun properly, he understood tactics. Daniel's team discussed their game plan for Game 2, while the Welshman looked on, glancing at his stopwatch now and then. Daniel said they must get Big Dave. Bill suggested running up to him and calling him a big jessie. While appealing, this seemed to have limited strategic value, as it was unlikely that the volunteer for this mission would get much farther than shouting 'big' before being despatched. Daniel had his mobile phone with him. He wondered about ordering a pizza to be delivered to Big Dave. This would confuse him, especially if the topping were obscure – say, pineapple and taramasalata with extra chocolate. But they didn't know the number of a local pizza delivery company, and the Welsh Adjudicator was giving nothing away. And besides, Game 2 would be over before the pizza arrived.

Philip suggested that they all pretend to be dead.

By the time Daniel's team had lost Game 4, his mind was beginning to wander. It was five hours since he'd seen Katie, and he couldn't wait to see her again. As he and

Harry hid behind a tree, he confided, 'I'm not used to being like this. Is this love?' Harry, who was taking the game somewhat more seriously than his captain, scoured the forest looking for enemies. He fired.

'Love?' asked Harry as he reloaded. 'Because you haven't slept with her on the first date?' He dashed to another tree, then to another. Daniel followed. Harry fired and ducked back behind the tree.

Daniel was content to let Big Dave have his way in the Game, he had his mind on the other game. 'Second date. I'll push her tonight. It's crazy. She reads my mind. All I'm thinking about is having sex with her. OK, I admit it. But why? Because we're *not* having sex. I mean, once we've done it, I can forget about it.'

'Right,' said Harry, having emptied his pump action gun, and continued breathlessly, 'Once the challenge is over. The usual.'

Daniel warmed to this theme, 'This morning, thinking about her, the word nuzzle kept running through my head. Nuzzle, nuzzle, nuzzle.'

Harry got ready for his next round, and suggested, 'Maybe you should try and think of a similar word which is asexual.'

'Like what?'

'Err, nozzle,' replied Harry as he emptied a round into a nearby bush. Daniel considered.

'So, instead of thinking about nuzzling her breasts I think about nozzling them?'

They ducked, just in time to avoid a barrage of pellets that hit the tree behind them, and dashed through the wood, Harry trying to fend off any attackers with repeated shots into the undergrowth, Daniel scampering along with his gun waving in mid-air.

'So, screw her and end the relationship,' barked Harry.

'No, this is different,' insisted Daniel, holding his hands up (rifle included) to add emphasis. 'I mean, when have I ever been like this before?' They leapt through a puddle and scrambled into a ditch. 'I feel like I'm losing control.'

'How awful for you,' mocked Harry, peering over the top, then splatting a shrub with a load of pellets.

'The balance isn't right.'

'You mean it's not in your favour. Maybe you should go on one of your own courses.' As Harry kept firing, Daniel put down his gun and took his mobile phone out of his camouflage jumpsuit top pocket, and dialled.

Katie was in the little gallery section of her office, over her lab, where she did paperwork. She picked up the phone. She was pleased it was Daniel, but didn't want to show it too much.

'Oh, hi.' She smiled and swivelled her chair round.

'I can't make tonight,' lied Daniel.

'You can't?'

'Something's come up. I really am sorry.'

'OK.'

'You sound disappointed. Look, I'll try and —'

'No. No problem.'

'Well, another time maybe,' suggested Daniel, enjoying himself.

'Fine ... bye,' and she put the phone down. Another time? Maybe? And yet he'd been so keen this morning. Perhaps he'd lost interest because they hadn't ... well, fine, if that was the sort of person he was, she was better off without him.

Harry was looking at Daniel, shaking his head. 'You are quite unbelievable,' he said. 'Don't you have any scruples?' He thought of the games Daniel played. Like the time a girlfriend who he thought might be going cold went abroad. When she called him from the airport on her return, he had loud music playing in the background as if a party were going on, and when she said she was coming straight over, he quickly sprinkled cigarette butts on the carpet and hoovered them up, put lots of clean glasses in the dishwasher, and sprayed air freshener everywhere. Then another time he got Harry to call at midnight, let her answer it, and Harry put it down straight away. When it rang again next morning, she grabbed it, to find a girl asking for Daniel; it was Harry's daughter, Clare, so Daniel could feign total innocence.

The pressure was mounting in the woods. Daniel and Harry were aware the enemy were near. Daniel ran off along a line of trees, and Harry followed. They took cover in a gully.

'Of course I have scruples ...' purred Daniel, '... Watch.' He got out his phone and pressed the redial button. 'Hi, it's me. Look, I've managed to reschedule. Are you still on for tonight?'

'Yes,' said Katie, a little confused, but pleased nevertheless.

Harry saw some movement in a nearby bush, and shushed Daniel, who continued in a whisper, 'Great. Nine at my place. See you,' then switched off his phone. They had to keep everything to a whisper from now on, aware that the enemy were very close. 'See. I'm just restoring the balance,' hissed Daniel.

Harry replied in his best *sotto voce*, 'You're just manipulating her. You don't want to equal things out. You want to win.' As they peered round, searching for the slightest movement, Daniel pondered.

'How on earth do you win a relationship?' he asked.

Harry, his pump-action gun at the ready, and his eyeballs scampering from side to side in his goggles, explained as quietly as he could, 'Beat the opposition into submission.'

Brrrrrr-brrrrrrrrrrr, Daniel's phone rang. Their cover completely blown, Daniel and Harry were assailed by a torrent of paint pellets from four members of the Yellow team who'd been hovering over them, waiting for them to show.

'What?' asked Daniel, somewhat limply, unable to make out what was happening at the other end of his treacherous phone. It was Katie. Something about tonight. She'd be delayed. Already battered, this was a most bruising blow.

'But we agreed tonight. Later?' quizzed Daniel, unable to summon up the energy to counterattack. 'What time?' Harry listened to his friend, and smirked. Touché. Daniel wasn't pleased, but what could he do? She was talking about work and a colleague who'd just arrived from India. Hmmm. 'No, no, I understand. Don't worry. OK, bye.' He tried to make his parting sound sing-songy and carefree. Casual, even.

Having been 'got', they scrambled out of their hiding place, and strode through the undergrowth, towards the Neutral Zone, passing their assailants. Harry held up his arms over his head, as required by the rules. Daniel just walked through, fed up with the Game. One of the enemies observed, 'Oi, you're dead.'

Daniel, without stopping, grunted, 'I was faking,' and took the opportunity to empty a few rounds at his inter-locuter, something a dead player was definitely not allowed to do. Harry shrugged apologetically.

Katie had called Daniel as soon as she'd been buzzed by the porter, and told that she had a visitor. He'd probably just arrived that morning, and she wanted to hear all about the latest developments. Daniel could wait. She put down the phone, detecting more than a hint of irritation from his voice, and a great deal of pump-action gun being fired at close range. He'd told her what he was going to be doing today. She'd listened to his assertion that it was healthy, therapeutic, enlightening even, to be forced to live on your wits, responding to basic survival instincts, feeling primeval urges. And dressing up in cool outfits and being able to shoot guns at merchant bankers. She supposed it was harmless enough.

She looked down from her gallery as her visitor entered, peering round for her. 'Hey,' she said happily, and he looked up. Sandip, a handsome Indian man in his late forties, wearing a beige linen suit with a cashmere shawl wrapped over it, smiled. She scurried down the iron spiral staircase.

'How's my favourite psychic?' asked Sandip. She gave him a big hug. 'Careful, careful!' he admonished, as her hug was in danger of squashing the bundle of folded cotton he was clutching. She stepped back and excitedly took it from him, placing it on her bench, before carefully unfolding it to discover the little plastic sample bags it contained. Sandip looked on, delighted by his protegée's steady advancement in the academic world, and he felt proud to be standing in her very own lab at the Natural History Museum.

Her eyes ablaze with passion, she sifted through the samples of bones and fossils. 'Good?' asked Sandip as he wandered over to her.

'Where is she?' demanded Katie.

'She? Oh, you mean S 1762 G5.' He slowly produced a minute sample bag containing a tiny specimen from his top pocket. Gleefully, Katie took it and examined it carefully.

Daniel drove back to London with Harry in silence for most of the way. His team had been severely beaten. Big Dave was a titan, and only Bill the osteopath had managed to 'kill'. This had made Big Dave all the more angry, and, despite Bill's best efforts, time and again Daniel's flag had been confiscated and triumphantly taken back to Yellow base. Daniel's heart had not really been in it, although he had enjoyed running up to Big Dave and screeching 'big jessie' before a hail of pellets had rendered him extinct, at least for that game. They had managed to win one Game, but that had been by employing unusual and unrepeatable tactics. They had merely sat around their flag singing 'Ging-gang-gooly' until the enemy, somewhat confused by this, had come right up to them, while Bill drove off in one of the Adjudicator's Land Rovers and nabbed their flag.

Harry found it all rather amusing to see these financial types running around with muck on their faces. But now, as they approached the outskirts of London, he looked at Daniel, and offered, 'Look, you can't complain. If she was doing it to deliberately manipulate you, then you've found a soulmate, and if it was a genuine thing – if this guy really has just arrived from India – then you should be delighted she didn't cancel, that she's still coming.'

'Aaaeeh,' grunted Daniel in response, meaning 'I suppose you're right, but I'd still like her to drop everything'.

He dropped Harry off and stopped by the supermarket. She'd said, 'Later,' unsure how long she'd be with this colleague. Colleague? Old or young colleague? How long had she known him? Did he know about her 'secret'? Was he perhaps an old flame – the great love who'd made her so unwilling to commit herself to anyone else, and was now returning to claim his trophy?

He'd better make casserole. Something that wouldn't spoil if it had to wait. He bought some chicken breast fillets. And mushroom soup. And some cheap wine. Bung it all in, with healthy amounts of the latter, and call it chicken casserole. He bought salad. Yes, salad was good, it could wait. He'd often wondered about lettuce, though. Was it really worth the effort? Basically it was just water made barely solid and green, and merely afforded an excuse for dressing. But the energy involved in choosing a lettuce, buying it, taking it home, taking off the leaves (the outer ones were invariably slung straight into the bin for looking too manky or brown), washing it, drying it, putting it in a bowl, tossing it, putting it on your plate, picking it up with your fork, then putting it in your mouth for a second or so of taste, most of which came from the dressing, could scarcely be justified. He bought two cos lettuces.

He had a basket, so was able to go to the 'one basket only' checkout, which saved time. There were times, though, when he felt disapproving eyes looking at his bulging basket and the bottle of water in his hand, judging his shopping to be a small trolley's worth. But not today.

First on the conveyor belt was a charentais melon. Daniel wondered whether this was from the Charente, which, he'd read in a Sunday supplement, was on the Atlantic coast of France, but had a 'micro-climate' due to obscure conditions involving the Gulf Stream and some funny winds, thus making its weather more like that of Nice than adjacent areas. He'd been impressed. Caroline (as her badge announced), his checkout girl, however was unimpressed by the melon. 'Funny shape, isn't it? Sometimes I think they just grow things deliberately to give them funny shapes.' Daniel nodded. This was indeed an interesting theory. The supermarkets were, perhaps, under attack from neo-Situationists on both sides – the supplier and the consumer. Rogue shoppers had for years now been undermining the tyranny of the consumer society by taking, say, a packet of tomatoes and putting them temporarily in their trolley or basket, then placing them in the cheese fridge. Or planting a bottle of mouthwash with the frozen poultry.

There were also the part-time revolutionaries who contented themselves with putting cartons of milk in amongst the sweets and chocolates next to the checkouts. Perhaps, though, the funny shapes of vegetables were part of a wider marketing strategy . . .

'Melon, darling?'

'Oh, no thanks, the shape's too dull. Wait a second! Look at that one! What a great shape! Yes, yes, yes! We'll take six!'

. . . However, to Daniel, the charentais melon now being continually, but unsuccessfully, 'swiped' over that laser thing was very melon-shaped, not in the least surprising, but he had spotted on the vegetable counter some circular courgettes, shaped a bit like onions. They looked like they'd been squashed in a press, or had had an anvil land on them like unfortunate cartoon characters. Caroline was having such difficulty swiping the melon, that Daniel piped up that he thought they were on special offer, 99p. She believed him. He wished he'd said 89p.

At home, he had a shower, and succumbed to forty winks. He was pretty exhausted after all, having missed a night's sleep and having had to run around all day being fired on by venture capitalists. He lay down in a towel and shut his eyes. Then he thought he'd better set the alarm for eight-thirty p.m. just in case, but there was no way he wouldn't wake before that.

He awoke at eight-thirty, the clock-radio-alarm playing 'Frère Jacques' electronically. He'd bought it on the strength that it could play twelve tunes, including 'Boogie Nights' by Heatwave, but had so far failed to get from it anything other than 'Frère Jacques'. Lucy had found it intolerable and had pulled the plug out, so they'd relied on her own little alarm clock which could only offer the standard 'beep-beep-beep'. But she was gone and so was her clock.

119

Daniel awoke feeling very groggy. Having not fully dried his hair before lying down, Daniel now had a bad case of bedhead, clumps of hair pointing in different directions, giving him a look that would have been unseemly in a four-year-old, let alone a body language expert of thirty. He quickly had to wet it again, and then dry it while frying the chicken prior to putting it in the casserole dish with the soup and plenty of wine and a few spring onions and a dash of soy sauce, and – hey, why not? – a sprinkling of tarragon. By nine o'clock the casserole was chugging along, his hair was presentable, he was dressed in jeans, denim shirt and Timberland boots. He was set. But was the flat?

He adjusted the flame effect on his fire. It looked like a real fire, but was controlled by a little gas tap so you don't have to spend hours getting your hands all dirty rolling bits of newspaper and trying to get some reluctant coal, or wilfully damp wood to ignite. He looked around the living room. Good. Then he looked at one of the sofas. The ends of it – the sides, if you like, or arm rests, except they weren't arm rests because they were at neck height – were attached to the back with a cord with big tassels hooked over an ornate pointy thing, like a drawbridge you could raise or lower. With it lowered, you could rest your feet on it, and lie full length. Daniel lowered the drawbridge. He stopped and looked around. He dimmed the lights, then strode down the corridor to his bedroom and looked out into the street. Nothing.

He wandered back to the kitchen. There was a bottle of Sancerre, safely chilling in the fridge, but should he get some champagne on the go? He would normally. He reached to get one down from the rack above his fridge. He toyed with it, then decided against it. Not yet. If she was going to be late, she wouldn't get champagne. Anyway, maybe she'd think it was too much. Play it cool tonight.

His hand drifted down, and alighted on a yellow post-it note, on which he'd written 'US lecture – confirm dates'. He moved the magnetic piglet by which it was attached, so the note was easier to read. Next to it was a Virgin Atlantic airline ticket, held in place with a magnetic teddy bear. He sauntered back into the living room, and stood in the doorway for a moment, and pondered . . . drawbridge, dimmed lights, fire . . . ah, fire. He went to it, bent down to the little gas tap at the side, and turned it up. Get the place nice and warm. Just in case.

Back at her lab, Katie was engrossed in S 1764 G5. She prodded and pushed the tiny specimen as she examined it under the microscope. 'This is incredible,' she pronounced.

'You don't know the whole story. We did find others, not half a mile away.'

'Like her?'

'In many ways, yes. But she was the only one with these dental carbon traces. Evidently, her greater intellect caused the rest of the tribe a problem. They couldn't keep up with her. So she left.'

'Good girl. She got her priorities right.' Advancement. Progress. Cooked dinner.

The smell of the chicken casserole was wafting pleasantly through Daniel's apartment. He was pacing unpleasantly. It was after ten-thirty. She was very late. He had a quick look at the dinner. It was surviving, but he sloshed some more wine in, just to make sure it didn't get too dry. He took a gulp of wine himself. Ten bloody thirty. This was a very clever game she was playing.

Suddenly he remembered something, and rushed to the bathroom, and carefully felt for a very small, very private drawer. He gently pulled it out. Inside were a number of brand new, still-in-the-packet, light-blue toothbrushes, just like the one he'd chucked away on Lucy's departure. He took one and put it in the glass next to his own. The door bell went.

He hurried to the settee, and lay down, trying to make as much as an imprint as possible, as if he'd been lying there all evening, relaxing, rather than pacing around doing this and that and peering out of the window. He stayed where he was. It rang again. He got up, and casually opened the door.

Katie pushed her way in and pecked him on the cheek. Squeezing through just behind her, to Daniel's bewilderment, was Sandip.

'Sorry I'm late,' cried Katie, heading into the living room.

'It's my fault,' confessed Sandip, following her, leaving Daniel shutting the door weakly behind them.

Katie sat on the sofa, at the other end from the drawbridge, and explained, 'Daniel, this is Sandip. He's a genius. And a very old friend. He's brought over some fantastic bones from that site in India.'

'To eat?' asked Daniel, turning the dimmer switch on the lights to FULL ON.

'To study.'

Sandip took off his shawl and laid it on the other sofa before sitting. 'I hope I'm not intruding.'

Daniel waved a heavily carefree hand in the air, as Katie responded, 'Not at all.'

Daniel strode deliberately to the fire and turned it completely off, fixing Sandip with a stare, who said, 'I'll only stay for a quick drink. Then I'll be off. I have work to do in the morning.'

Daniel looked at Katie, then at Sandip, then put his hands on his hips, and showed his palms to the ceiling and said, 'Fine.' He sighed and enquired, 'Drink?'

'Whisky, please,' said Sandip.

122

'Good,' exclaimed Daniel, and headed off to the kitchen. Katie followed him, 'And I'll have white wine.'

'In the fridge, there's one open,' barked Daniel. She could have that cheap old Italian stuff he'd opened at the weekend. Somebody had brought it to a dinner party three months before and it had lain unwanted until Daniel had fancied spicing up some late-night mushrooms on toast. She could have that if she was going to bring along old Sandpit or whatever his name was. Good job he hadn't got the champagne ready. What a cheek. Katie brought out the pariah bottle from the fridge, while Daniel sought ice cubes in the freezer compartment below. He stood up and observed, 'Sandip seems very nice,' thinking he seems a randy old bastard, but moving away from her so she couldn't read this thought.

'He's the leading man in his field,' assured Katie, then spotted the yellow post-it note. US lecture tour? Must be soon if he had the ticket already. How soon?

Daniel was retrieving some glasses from the dishwasher. 'He certainly looks like a genius,' remarked Daniel as he swilled them out. Katie came over to him and took a wine-glass.

'Platonic, of course?'

'Right. Platonic. He's only interested in –'

'– Your mind?' interrupted Daniel, chucking some ice in two glasses. 'Look,' he lowered his voice, 'I may not have ESP, but I recognise bullshit when I hear it. He's after you. It's in his eyes.'

'Nonsense, I'd have noticed.'

'Just watch him.' He poured two whiskies. 'You read his mind, I'll read his body. We'll compare notes.'

'No,' hissed Katie, but Daniel had gone into the living room.

Daniel smiled as he handed over the drink. Sandip, his

legs crossed, watched him sit on the sofa with a smile. Daniel scrutinised Sandip, and said, 'So, how long have you known Katie?' crossing his legs. Katie came and sat next to Sandip.

'Three, four years. It seems much longer.' Daniel's eyes darted up and down Sandip, who somewhat uneasily looked down to see what had attracted Daniel's attention, wondering if he had brought in something undesirable on his shoe. Sandip looked at Katie, uncrossed his legs and continued, 'We've achieved so much.' Daniel leant forward, trying to look as though he was listening intently, but keeping his eyes on Sandip's legs as he now crossed them the other way. 'And there's so much more to do,' Sandip ploughed on, despite Daniel's close inspection. 'That's why this grant is so important.' He took a sip of whisky. Daniel put his to his mouth, while still keeping an eye on Sandip. Then he realised what he'd just heard.

'Grant? What grant?'

Sandip waved a loose hand as he explained, 'It's a private endowment to finance research in the field of palaeontology.'

'Fifty thousand pounds,' added Katie, hoping to shift some of the limelight from Sandip.

But Sandip took her hand, and proudly proclaimed, 'We are on the shortlist,' and gave the back of Katie's hand a little kiss.

'Really?' said Daniel, leaning gently back and crossing his legs, in the opposite way from Sandip.

Sandip took a little sip before getting up. 'Well, I'd better be going.' He headed to the front door, as Katie glared at Daniel. He put his shawl on over his suit.

Katie said, 'Goodbye,' accompanied by a little peck, and he opened the door and left. Daniel raised his hand in a half-hearted wave. As the door shut, he immediately went into conciliatory mode.

'OK. OK. I was wrong. His body language was almost asexual. Tactile but asexual.' He retreated to the kitchen.

Katie followed, 'Exactly.'

As Daniel opened the oven to reveal the casserole pot, he asked, 'So what was he thinking?'

She leant against the dishwasher, saying, 'I'm not sure. It was in Indian ... *Jee chahta hai ley* something.' Daniel, with the aid of an ovenglove, laid his evening's work on the hob.

Katie looked at it and said, 'Actually, I'm not hungry.' Daniel started, and she added, 'I'm tired.'

'OK, I'll give you a lift home.'

'No, it's all right. I'll stay here.' Daniel was surprised. 'If that's all right with you.'

'Sure.'

'I thought it might be.' Daniel kissed her. A long slow kiss on the lips.

She didn't resist, but then said, 'There will be no sex.'

'That's a relief.'

'And no fondling.'

'Excellent.' His eyes wandered down her body.

'And whatever nozzling is, there'll be none of that either.'

He looked at the casserole, and left it where it was. He turned the oven off, and looked at her. His eyes indicated the direction of the bedroom. She smiled. He took her hand and led her down the corridor, then opened the door for her. She went in ahead of him, he followed and shut the door.

Daniel tentatively edged towards her. She was facing away from him, but she sensed him and said, 'Yes, you can,' in a sing-songy voice. He stood right behind her and reached around her shoulders and began unbuttoning her beige linen shirt. As he gently undid one button after the

125

other, she tenderly gripped his left wrist, and turned round to face him. They kissed, a passionate, squidgy kiss. Sufficient buttons had been undone for him now to be able to calmly let her shirt drop, revealing one shoulder, then the other. Through the corner of his eye, he saw a white bra. His hands were heading to the back of it, wondering if she'd mind, when she said, 'No, it's a front catch.' Thank you, he thought, and undid it.

He started concentrating on the side of her neck, delicately kissing, wondering whether he could nuzzle soon. His tongue played along her shoulder. She smelt good. What about him? Had he put on too much aftersh –?'

'– Don't worry about your aftershave,' she reassured him.

Thank you, he thought, as she confidently undid his shirt and let it drop. Oh no, he thought, she's going to see my chest, what if –

'No, I like hairy chests,' she said, right on cue. He was beginning to want to start the attack on all fronts. 'I'm glad you trimmed your nails.'

Encouraged, he kissed his way across her face, and began concentrating on her other shoulder, then worked his way back into her neck. He thought about moving upwards, knowing this to be a highly sensitive area; the moment could be ruined if she found it too ticklish, or it could send her into passionate oblivion.

'Yes . . . blow in my ear!' she gasped. He moved round and down her neck, and she screamed, 'Yes. Nozzle. Nozzle now.'

He did.

Soon they were in bed, or on it anyway, naked, making love.

She was thinking, 'Is this how he makes love to other women? Am I any different? Does he love me? Do I love him?' Just then Daniel moved, slowly, firmly, pulling himself up the bed, making her gasp. 'Oh God, that feels good!' she thought. 'Now where was I?'

'This is incredible,' he said.

She opened her eyes, 'What?'

'Everything ... I think ... you do,' he stammered, his mind opening up to the possibilities.

'Don't push your luck,' she chided. He headed towards her ear, she moved her head to help him, but he stopped short.

'See, you knew I was going to –' She put her fingers to his lips and silenced him. 'Doesn't that make it less exciting?' He stroked her face, but she said nothing. 'Well?'

She looked into his eyes, and said, 'I can do this,' and closed her eyes.

'That works?'

'Yes. That works,' she whispered. Daniel smiled wickedly, and gently moved his thighs from side to side. 'Yes. Yes,' she cried, and so he continued. 'Yes ... Yes ... Yes ... Yes,' she cried, as Daniel considered the revelation that shutting her eyes cut off her ESP.

Chapter Eight

It was half past nine when they awoke, without the aid of 'Frère Jacques'. Katie was horrified – normally she was up by eight. 'But it's a Saturday!' pointed out Daniel. Apparently that made no difference. So he leapt up, and told her to stay where she was. He threw on a tee-shirt and jeans and put the kettle on, and headed out to get some croissants from the shop down the road. He almost skipped along, such was his satisfaction with the night's proceedings. If this is what having a girlfriend with ESP meant, he could handle it.

When he got back to the flat, far from having stayed where she was, she had filled the coffee percolator and put last night's chicken casserole in a dish in the fridge. She took him by the hand and led him to the bedroom. He wasn't sure if he was ready for a repeat performance yet, without any breakfast, but she indicated the clock-radio-alarm, and pressed a button. Some tinny electronic sounds came out, and he tried to nod along, but then, after a few bars, he recognised 'Boogie Nights'. Just.

He kissed her, and asked, 'Are you busy today? Have you got anything planned?'

'I – er –' But he wouldn't let her finish.

'Good. Because I want you to meet my very good friends Harry and Caroline. And their daughter Clare. Well, you've met Harry. Briefly. Those were his notes that you knocked out of my hand the second time you punched me.'

'All right, but I need a couple of hours at home. To organise a few things.'

'Sandip?'

'No, I'm not seeing him till Monday. He has other friends and colleagues. So do I.'

'OK, I'll take you home now – you can freshen up, whatever, then we'll pick you up this afternoon. We're taking Clare swimming. At this pool, there's a waterchute – you can swim, can't you?'

'Fine. OK.'

Once he dropped her, he dashed home and called Harry. 'Now you can decide for yourself. You can see the ESP in action.'

'Daniel? Is this you?'

'Yes. Look, I'm bringing her with me – swimming.'

'I'd better warn Caroline. And Clare,' gulped Harry.

Harry and Daniel had to wait for Caroline and Katie to emerge from the changing room, but when they did Harry gave a little wink to Daniel. Katie looked terrific in her one-piece black swimsuit. Clare was desperate to be zooming down the chute – the Wet 'n' Wild Tube. Daniel took her up first. Harry didn't really like the waterchute, he found it a bit scary, and had managed to perfect a technique with his ankles that reduced his speed of descent to one which he could handle comfortably. He took Clare down, Caroline followed, then Harry, then Katie, whose feelings about it were similar to Harry's. Daniel was soon at the top again, but waited for Caroline and Clare, who then went down together. Katie and Harry slowly climbed up, unenthusiastically, then down. They were both thinking that two descents were quite sufficient to demonstrate team spirit, when Clare padded up to them and demanded that 'Daddy and Uncle Danny's new bird' take her down. Harry looked at Katie and, even without ESP he knew this would be their last trip down. Caroline and Daniel preceded them, laughing and screeching. Katie and Harry

129

gingerly prepared to go down, with Harry holding Clare firmly between his legs.

In between squeals, Caroline shouted to Daniel, 'Do you think they're enjoying themselves?'

'I doubt it,' laughed Daniel.

'How long do you think it'll last?'

'I don't knowwwwwwwwwwwwoah!' And they flopped into the water.

Caroline stood up first, and giggled, 'Well, you can't complain that she doesn't understand the real you.' Daniel grimaced and splashed her. She splashed him back and they headed out of the pool and onwards and upwards for another Wet 'n' Wild journey.

To the annoyance of other would-be chuters, Harry, Katie and Clare's descent was one of the slowest on record, and as they approached the bottom, Harry let Clare go, and reached out so that both his palms touched the side, thus virtually destroying all the good work that gravity had been doing on him from the top of the chute. But Katie didn't mind. She was happy to avoid another noseful of chlorine.

As they found their feet, and rearranged their hair, Harry pointed to the café and asked her, 'Listen, you don't want a —'

'I'd love one.' Harry gave a little nod. Ah-ha.

Harry and Katie emerged a few minutes later, dry and dressed. Well, dressed anyway, it was hard to get your hair dry, especially when all that was available was one of those hand dryers, activated when you put your hand underneath, and only then if you put it the right way — the right way being known only to Freemasons and attendants whose smugness knows no bounds when, having told them that you can't get it to work, they calmly put a hand underneath and it works instantaneously. These are not easy for drying hair. You look stupid, you may burn your ear, and you certainly won't dry your hair in an even, stylish manner. You look more like you've had an electric shock, or one side is dry and wispy and the other is still soaking wet.

Anyway, both had wet hair. Harry's was much drier – he had less of it, and a vigorous towel movement would do eighty per cent of what was required, but he had a slightly wet back – it was so difficult to know when your back was dry; you only really knew once you put your shirt on and felt that clammy patch.

They headed to the café area, and Harry made funny noises to Clare as he carried her.

Katie spoke to the girl behind the counter. 'One decaf coffee, black, no sugar –'

'Make that two,' said Harry.

'No. It's *for* you. And a coke for Clare.' The assistant turned round to make the coffee, as Katie asked, 'Is the orange juice freshly squeezed?' The assistant didn't turn round. Angrily Katie chided, 'Well, it should be.' The assistant looked round surprised. 'And there's no need to swear,' Katie was getting rather heated, so Harry stepped in.

'Look, I'll get these,' he said, as Katie went to a table. He explained to the assistant, 'She's got ESP.'

'I hope it's not catching,' grunted the assistant.

Harry walked over, still carrying Clare, who commented, 'She's a very strange lady, isn't she, Daddy.'

'I'd really rather not think about it, Clare.' Harry was smiling at Katie as they headed toward her table.

Clare chirped, 'And her bosoms are bigger than Mummy's.' Harry, noticing Clare looking at Katie's chest, had a quick glance himself before swiftly changing direction, heading to the Kiddies' Area to despatch his garrulous daughter.

131

Harry took a deep breath and sat opposite Katie. He plunged in with, 'You know, you've made quite an impression on Daniel. I've never seen him like this.' She looked hard at him. She knew he was thinking about all the others. And there had clearly been plenty of them. But Daniel couldn't treat her as just another. This would have to be a grown-up relationship.

Katie told Harry, 'I just find him . . . childish.'

'He is childish. Most men are childish. I'm childish. I brought home a picture that Daniel painted just before he met you. I got Caroline to tell Daniel that it looked like a child cast adrift on an endless ocean. It looked nothing like it.'

Katie supped her orange juice, wincing at its slightly stale taste.

'Anyway, it worked,' added Harry. 'He went along to the dating agency. He met you.'

Harry saw something out of the corner of his eye. 'I think we're meant to watch this.' Katie turned and saw that Caroline and Daniel were waving from the stairs leading to the top of the chute. Harry waved back unenthusiastically, a look of adulterated pleasure on his face. Katie just looked.

Harry kept waving, and muttered, 'I don't do this with my own child.'

Caroline and Daniel finished waving, and climbed on up.

Harry turned back to Katie, and wiped the fixed grin off his face. Katie didn't have one to wipe and complained, 'But he doesn't treat the relationship seriously.'

'Well, that doesn't mean he's not serious.'

'Is that why he's planning a trip to the States?' This was news to Harry.

'He hasn't said anything to me.'

'Exactly.'

After one more go down the chute, Daniel and Caroline went and got changed and they all headed for Harry and Caroline's Range Rover. Daniel used to tease Harry that it was only people who lived in Camden, Chelsea and Holland Park who drove Range Rovers and their ilk – land cruisers, jeeps, action vehicles, troopers, four-wheel drives – and that people who lived in the country were quite happy driving ordinary saloon cars. Harry said it was useful as a family car, and Daniel readily agreed – of course, you need all that extra storage space and big wheels with one five-year-old. Harry gave up trying to win the argument.

Caroline drove, with Harry next to her in the front seat, Daniel behind him, Katie behind Caroline and Clare in the middle of them. They were playing a mind-reading game to test Katie's powers. They were all thinking hard of Daniel's birthday.

'First of June 1962,' announced Katie.

'Amazing,' said Caroline, amazed. 'OK – our wedding anniversary.'

'Tenth of May, eighty-nine, according to you. Harry thinks it's the ninth.'

'Because it is the ninth,' insisted Harry, leaning over his seat to look at Katie.

'It's the tenth,' said Daniel, who'd been best man, and had had that date emblazoned on his mind for the preceding six months.

Caroline gave Harry an affectionate smile, 'Useless.'

Daniel asked, 'OK, who's up for a bite?'

'I am,' announced Katie.

'Me too,' chimed in Caroline. 'Where shall we go, Harry? Harry?' Caroline undid her seat belt.

Harry was distracted, 'What?'

Then Katie said, 'Actually, on second thoughts, no.'

'Why not?' asked Caroline, feeling it would be a good chance to get to know Katie better. 'It'll be fun.'

'It's all right,' murmured Katie, staring at Harry. An air of tension filled the car. Daniel didn't know what to make of it. Katie had suddenly changed her mind. Didn't she like his friends?

'You don't have to eat,' he told her. Clare sucked her thumb, oblivious.

'What about you, Harry?' asked Caroline.

'No, he's . . . really . . . tired,' ejaculated Katie.

'Are you, Harry?' enquired Caroline.

He didn't look that tired, but he looked a bit confused, and could only manage an, 'Err . . . well,' and a wave of the hand in response.

'Fine. No problem,' muttered Caroline, doing up her seat belt tetchily.

Katie looked at Caroline, 'No. It's not fine. You're annoyed. You want to go out.'

But Caroline wanted to close the matter, 'I've said it's no problem.'

Daniel looked at Katie, and thrust his door open. Katie opened hers and got out. Daniel glared at her then leaned over and gave Caroline a kiss and patted Harry's shoulder, and whispered, 'Sorry.' He kissed Clare goodbye and headed to the front door of his building, where Katie was waiting, looking at her feet. He said nothing and waved off the Range Rover, before opening the door and heading up the stairs to his flat.

Daniel wanted Katie to know he was riled, and let her stew as he opened the door. Katie felt she had no need to be defensive, and calmly said, 'I only told the truth.'

But nobody asked you for the truth, thought Daniel,

they asked if you were hungry. 'You can't go around open-ing up people's minds like that. No wonder you've got no friends.'

'I can't help it,' she snarled, as she rummaged in the fridge. Now she was defensive. 'This is how I am. Every time I meet people, I see through to the core. All their fears, their inner misery.'

'Misery?' Pompous cow, he was thinking, and didn't care if she knew it. He opened the fridge door, before pointing out to her, 'He was tired!'

'If you say so,' she said in a sing-song voice before head-ing to the living room with a small bar of chocolate.

Daniel grabbed a loaf of bread and cut into it with a sharp knife with great gusto. 'I mean, really, Katie, you've got to find a way of living without upsetting people all the time. Or hitting them.' He enjoyed that.

She glared at him from the sofa, 'You expect me to be easy-going like you?' She imbued 'easy-going' with great distaste, as if saying 'puke'.

'Why not? Really, why not? I've worked at it. I've trained myself to deal with situations so that I get what I want.' Accompanying this, he joined his right forefinger and thumb and drew them from his head to his navel, his 'centre', a move which his body language lecturer at Harry Porter University, West Carolina, had used. It had im-pressed Daniel greatly and he frequently pilfered it, to good effect, he thought.

He'd finished making his cheese sandwich. The bread was a little thicker than he would have preferred, but that was a result of cutting in anger, never a good idea. He grasped his food and headed into the living room, explain-ing to her, 'There's nothing to it. You could learn. It might help . . .' He triumphantly shoved the sandwich in his gob.

She looked at him, and took a delicate bite of chocolate.

She contemplated what he had said. Maybe he could teach her something. She'd already upset three people today – the café assistant, Harry and Caroline. And her mother had always told her she had to control her temper. She had to understand that people didn't always mean what they thought. Hmmm.

After a few minutes of silent eating, during which time Daniel chomped away and perused the TV pages to see what was on, Katie suddenly said, 'OK.'

'What?'

'OK, you can teach me. Train me to deal with situations without upsetting people or hitting them. Teach me harmonious personal relations in the social interface or whatever.'

'You've got to take it seriously.'

'Yes. I'll even pay you.'

'What?'

'In kind.'

'Sounds good.'

'Mmmm.'

'No more talk of bullshit psychology?'

'Promise.'

Daniel decided their first task must be to try and make amends at Angelino's. It was, after all, Daniel's favourite restaurant, and he couldn't show his face there as things stood. Katie wasn't sure. Daniel persuaded her it was exactly the right place to go. If they could win Vincenzo back they could do anything.

It was early evening, so it wasn't properly open yet. Paolo was setting tables. He had a plaster on his forehead. When he looked up to see who'd just come in and saw Katie and Daniel, he dropped the silverware and fearfully scurried off to see the boss, to tell him of the approaching violence.

'Just trust me,' said Daniel to Katie. He'd told her all about copy behaviour. Follow what your foe does, crossing arms, looking left, touching your nose, or whatever, and he or she will become your friend, unaware of the subtle manipulation.

'You just copy everything?' she asked, still incredulous.

'That's it,' replied Daniel, enjoying being her teacher, and hopeful of an oyster or two on the house.

'Won't he notice?' she wanted to know – surely anyone would realise if you were doing exactly the same as them.

'We'll see.'

Vincenzo came scuttling over. 'No, no, no, no. Signor Becker, please, sorry. You are not welcome here. Sorry, sorry.'

'But why? asked Daniel, exuding affable reasonableness.

'You know why. And she knows why.'

'Look, you must let me explain,' whispered Daniel, leading him away into a corner, away from Katie.

'I cannot afford such an incident,' said Vincenzo. His restaurant was for the gourmet, not the all-in wrestler, and to emphasise the point he poked himself in the chest with his forefinger, and finished with a flourish of the palm in the air.

Daniel did exactly the same as he responded, 'I understand,' with great feeling.

'It is bad for business,' explained Vincenzo, his hands begging to be believed. Katie stared, dumbfounded.

Daniel used his hands in saying, 'You have a reputation.' Paolo the waiter came near Katie, carrying a plate to a nearby trolley, each highly aware of the other's presence.

'She is very sorry,' apologised Daniel, as Vincenzo crossed his arms, and Daniel followed suit. So did Paolo as he looked on, hoping Vincenzo wouldn't budge. Katie caught sight of him, so she crossed hers.

137

'*I* am very sorry,' insisted Daniel; Vincenzo, my dear, dear, old friend, he tried to communicate, as he looked him deep in the eye. Vincenzo was no match for this. A smile spread across his face, his arms unfolded, and he said, 'Ah well, *va bene*, in that case,' and spread his arms in a pre-hug gesture, which Daniel imitated, then clapped them together, as did Daniel. Big smiles, as they looked over to see what the noise was. Paolo was prostrate. Katie stood over him, nursing her fist. No more smiles.

'He was at it again,' exclaimed Katie, in mitigation.

Daniel marched over to her, and, without breaking his stride, stepped over the horizontal waiter, grabbed her and they were on their way out. Lesson One was a disaster and Daniel was livid. He shouted, 'That was —'

'— So stupid. I know.' For once he was glad of her finishing his sentence.

'Look I really have no idea how —'

'I know, I know.'

She was ashamed. The very thing she was supposed to avoid — acting on impulse based on others' unarticulated thoughts — she had done. And with a vengeance. It would be a very, very long time before Daniel could see himself tucking into a nice plate of oysters at Angelino's, and even then only with St John's Ambulance standing by.

It had been a very simple request, an easy assignment — for her anyway. We go to a restaurant and you don't hit the waiter. Not difficult. And he was going to try and get it through to her that they had no future unless she could deal with this. He didn't want to have to spend the rest of his life adding another column next to gratuities, for hospital bills, when paying the bill in restaurants.

They walked across Richmond Bridge in silence. She knew what he was thinking, and he knew she knew, but that didn't make it any better. Halfway across he looked at her, and she said, 'I know.' But that wasn't good enough.

'You may know, but I'd be grateful if you'd let me tell you anyway.' He stopped suddenly and stared at her, making her stop, 'Close your eyes.'

'What?'

'Exasperated, he covered her eyes with his hand, took a big breath, and launched into, 'Right. I really have no idea how you expect to have a relationship with *anyone*. Going out with you is like being an accomplice on an assault and battery charge. Can you imagine what would happen if we went to the theatre? They'd have to put every hospital within fifty miles on standby. If we go abroad I'll have to notify the International Red Cross.'

He took his hand away, but she kept her eyes closed. Their foreheads touched. He went on, 'Everyone has thoughts they can't help. You've got to learn to live with it, Katie.' He knew he'd been hard, and he gave her a conciliatory kiss. 'OK. Speech over. You can open them.'

'I'm not sure I want to.'

He grasped her elbows. 'Open them, Katie.'

But she kept them firmly shut, 'No really, I mean it. It's easier.' He smiled and stroked her hair. She walked on over the bridge, and Daniel had to dash to grab her before she bumped into an old lady. He guided her along, all the way back to his car.

They went back to his flat, and Daniel put his coal-fire-effect gas fire on straight away, and soon they were making reckless love in front of it. Katie wore a blindfold, made out of one of Daniel's thicker ties.

The next day was Sunday, and Katie wanted it to herself. Daniel didn't want to push, so he made a date with her for Monday. He spent the day catching up; he did washing, checking his diary and bills, and phoning friends. He called Harry and Caroline to apologise. They were fine about it, Harry saying it was always sticky early at the start of a relationship but he couldn't imagine what it must be like to have ESP. Daniel agreed it did lead to difficulties, but that the use of a blindfold curtailed these. 'Really?' said Harry, intrigued. 'What about handcuffs?'

'Goodbye, Harry,' said Daniel and put the phone down, before having a small plateful of reheated chicken casserole and getting an early night.

The next day Katie was working at her lab, with Sandip alongside her, both looking into separate microscopes. She was taking a closer look at the specimens he had. 'These are really fascinating. Early Neanderthal,' she said, without looking up.

'How is Daniel?' asked Sandip, also intently looking down his microscope. Katie raised her eyes, and smiled as she pondered what to say.

'Hmmmm . . . Lovable.'

Sandip still didn't look up, but asked, 'You love him?'

She twiddled with the microscope, before saying, 'We think so differently I'm not sure. But the feeling –'

Sandip cut her off, still intent on his microscope, 'Look at this.' Katie went over to Sandip's microscope, and looked into it.

'Where's it from?' she asked.

'The skull of our friend.' S 1762 G5. Near his microscope was a completed reconstruction of the skull. Sandip referred to it, speaking profoundly, 'See how her brain was constricted by the bone. The more we use our brains over time the more the size of the skull increases. Each generation has a duty to develop the intellect, to push back this piece of bone. To be –'

'– Pioneers,' Katie interrupted: this wasn't the first time she'd heard this, and she didn't feel like hearing it again.

He sighed, and, as Katie headed back to her microscope, 'There are so few of us left,' he said and stared intently into his microscope.

She sat at her seat, and asked, 'Have you found out any more about India?'

'If we win the grant, I don't think there will be a problem. What about Daniel? Have you told him?' They both knew the ramifications. If they got the grant, Katie would have to go to India very soon and not return for six months at least, maybe a year or two.

She didn't look up from her microscope, and answered, 'Not yet. Anyway, he's planning a trip to the States. And he hasn't told me.'

'Isn't that a bit childish?'

She turned and looked at him with a cheeky smile, 'Yes. I suppose it is.' She enjoyed the feeling of mischief, despite Sandip's apparent disapproval of this unseen side of her. Pausing for a moment to summon up courage, she said, 'Can I ask you a question?'

Sandip gazed up at her, 'Of course.'

'What does *Jee chahta hai ley loon tumhare shebaab kaa russ* mean?' She felt somewhat nervous. She'd read his thoughts before, but had never understood, and had never had the courage to ask for a translation. She had always been too overawed. When he'd found her crying one day, after the break-up with Gordon, her secret had come out. She felt comfortable that he knew, and could confide in him in a way that she couldn't with others, men or women. But she wanted to know what he'd been thinking that day, because he was thinking it now. She'd only ask this once, feeling rather strange, but at least this way she could report back to Daniel how innocent it had all been.

Sandip looked her straight in the eye, and said, 'It must be confusing for you to read someone's thoughts in another language. It means "My stomach is empty".' They laughed.

'Mine too. Let's get some lunch,' said Katie.

Chapter Nine

That evening Daniel had told her he would pick her up at seven and that she should dress formally; he was going to be in black tie. Katie wasn't sure about this – she didn't really like too much formality and couldn't stand those big dinners where you want to stop eating and go home half-way through the main course but have to continue nibbling and chatting to some twerp as he gets more and more drunk. Daniel assured her it would be nothing like that.

At seven, the doorbell rang, she took a quick nibble of chocolate and headed downstairs. He looked good in his tuxedo, and he gave a sigh of admiration as he surveyed her in her long black dress. She laughed it off but was pleased by his approval. They drove for twenty minutes and pulled up outside a beautiful Georgian house on one of those one-way roads between Baker Street and Regent Street, which Katie had only ever been down in taxis as they avoided traffic on Marylebone High Road around Madame Tussaud's, but would never have dared drive down on her own for fear of getting horribly lost. A silver plaque outside it announced that it was the Institute of Applied Psychology. Next door a blue plaque told passers-by that the house had once been the home of Sir Anthony Gordon Hawksworth, actor-manager and gentleman, between 1878 and 1896.

As they went in, Katie was taken aback by the beauty of the place. The circular foyer, with its mosaic floor, led on to an ornate curved staircase, and everywhere there were oil paintings of old codgers who, in fact, turned out to be leading figures in the history of applied psychology. Daniel explained that he'd got a mate to recommend him for membership, and that for three hundred quid a year you could come and lunch whenever you liked – cheap but cosy, meat and two veg, school-dinner style – and could book the function rooms very cheaply. It had one of the finest wine cellars this side of Harley Street, but was crumbling. Apart from the foyer and staircase, and the main function room, the building was in a dire state. The smaller rooms gave off that smell which is only earned after years of neglect, and needed several licks of paint. The carpets, mostly brown or purple, had last been renewed when Flintlock were still in the charts. But he loved it. Every fortnight or so, there would be a lecture on such subjects as 'The Psychosexuality of Subbuteo', 'The Taxonomy of Personality; towards a new Heuristics of the Aetiology of Prototypicality', and 'Soap Operas – Good or Bad?'

There was also a recital every month or so, where, for no good reason, members would dress in dinner jackets and gowns and listen to some piano music, string quartet or, as tonight, a harpsichordist. Daniel thought this might appeal to Katie. He had, however, fearful of the potentially dangerous thoughts of his fellow members, been to Liberty's and bought a small piece of black material. Much to the irritation of the assistant who sold it to him, Daniel had not given away its intended use. So, as they sat down, and Katie's eyes danced suspiciously around the room, he offered it to her. She nodded with a grin and put it on as a blindfold. A grey-haired man next to Daniel, an eminent academic in the field of cognitive dissonance, whom Daniel had once seen fall down the ornate curved stairs when completely pissed, looked askance. Daniel whispered by way of explanation, 'To appreciate the music better,' which got a nod of understanding.

The blindfold turned out to have many uses, not all of them indoors. Katie enjoyed the new-found freedom it gave her. That weekend, they went walking on Hampstead Heath, and found themselves in the colonnades where they'd been when they walked all night. They played a game of blind man's buff. Daniel would tease Katie with the occasional 'over here', she would follow his voice, and he'd kiss her then dart away. He had a packet of monkey nuts, and planted one in her mouth, before scuttling off. Then he rounded a corner, and saw a squirrel. He put a nut on the floor, and it scampered over. Daniel gave the squirrel a feast, and gently called Katie over. He'd had an idea, and slowly guided Katie down to where he was. Using a nut as bait he guided the squirrel to Katie. It jumped on her leg, he put the nut in her hand, and she squealed and took off the blindfold as she felt the little teeth nibbling from her palm. They both giggled and she hugged him.

One night they cooked together. She knew her way round his kitchen now, and had brought round some ingredients from home. Daniel also found in the bathroom a bag of bits and bobs – face cleanser, moisturiser and cotton wool balls – for a girl needs more than a toothbrush if she's to stay regularly. For the meal she'd bought some delicious home-made pesto sauce from the Positano deli. After eating, she put on her blindfold and they danced. Daniel watched her, thinking she looked very sexy, swaying her hips, dressed in jeans, white shirt and black blindfold. But for a moment, Daniel wasn't sure. Was he prepared to give up his independence for this girl? Yes. They got on brilliantly, in every respect – but did he love her? Would he be able to cope with the times when she didn't have the blindfold on? She'd snapped a bit at him earlier when it had briefly crossed his mind that she was putting too much vinegar in the salad dressing. He forgot about it as she danced back to him and kissed him lusciously on the lips.

That night, he couldn't sleep too well. He got up, hot and bothered, and questions ran through his mind. If he wasn't sure, what about her? Was she thinking this was the big one or was she more sensible than that? Was she just playing along? She'd told him that she'd asked Sandip what he'd been thinking that night. Why had she bothered to do that? Wasn't she sure it was just platonic? Had she hoped that it had meant something more than just 'my stomach is empty'? Sandip, after all, might be more suitable for her: calm, intellectual, and, with their work, they had so much more in common. She hadn't really changed her mind about Daniel being a bullshit psychologist, had she? He went back to bed, and kept glancing over at the clock-radio- alarm, wishing that 'Frère Jacques', or 'Boogie Nights' would come on soon. Eventually at seven-thirty in the morning, he gave up and went into the living room to put on Mozart's *Requiem*. Loud.

He stood in his dressing-gown, staring out the window, just as he'd done with Lucy. And the others. He needed to know what to do. See how she responded. Was she serious? Was he serious?

He heard her get up and go to the bathroom. He kept looking out of the window, until she emerged, dressed. She strode up to him, gave him a kiss, said, 'Don't be silly,' squeezed his earlobe and headed off to work. The front door banged shut before Daniel could work out what had happened. He used the remote to turn off the music, and touched his ear, still trying to make sense of it. She'd obviously read his thoughts and dismissed them. She hadn't stormed out in high dudgeon; she hadn't begged him to stay; she'd just said, 'Don't be silly.' What had he been thinking? 'Maybe I can't handle the commitment,' or something like that. He hadn't had to say anything like that when Lucy left. His silence had been enough. But now

Katie had just laughed it off with a kiss and a squeeze of the ear. She was different.

He got dressed and drove to work. He zipped up the stairs and went straight to Harry's room. Harry was practising his juggling, which he liked doing when he thought one side (Daniel couldn't remember which) of his brain had been doing too much and things needed evening up. He started when Daniel burst in, but couldn't say anything before Daniel held up his hand, and marched straight into the darkened Therapy Room. Harry continued with his juggling, realising that Daniel needed to be alone. He left it twenty minutes. He made himself a coffee. Still Daniel didn't come out. Harry knocked on the door. No response. He did a bit more juggling, then knocked again. 'Finished yet?' Nothing. So he gingerly opened the door.

Daniel was painting eagerly, with long, flowing brush strokes, trying not to be a child cast adrift on an endless ocean. What was she doing? . . . Don't be silly, indeed! He was aware of Harry slipping in next to him. The silence endured for a few moments before Daniel muttered, 'She told me not to be silly.'

'Hmm?'

'I put on Mozart's *Requiem* and she told me not to be silly.'

'So?' Harry wasn't sure what this meant; he had a vague recollection of Daniel telling him his chucking technique, and it involving Mozart's *Requiem*.

'So . . . she's supposed to get angry and –'

'– And what? Leave?'

'No!' shouted Daniel. 'No, that's not what I want.'

'So you should be happy.'

'Yeah, well I am happy!' snapped Daniel.

'Oh,' observed Harry, not wanting to point out the incongruity between his alleged happiness and his obvious state of tension. He let it rest. Daniel painted on.

146

Harry took a breath and innocently asked, 'When do you go to the States?' Ah, thought Daniel, that's what they were talking about at the swimming pool. He had been a little nervous, leaving Katie with his best friend, who might have been unable to control his thoughts and give who knows what away. He'd hoped it had all been fairly perfunctory. She'd asked Harry about the note on the fridge . . . but she hadn't asked Daniel yet. What did this mean?

'I'm not going to the States.'

Harry didn't follow. 'But Katie said –'

'I always, always, leave a note on the fridge. The idea of a deadline adds spice to a relationship.' Harry leant back and sighed. That really was something: to have a permanent prop in your kitchen, just there to fool any girl, to 'add spice', seemed so Machiavellian that it took his breath away. And yet, the arch-conniver seemed to have met his match. He couldn't manipulate Katie. She was one step ahead of him and hadn't reacted at all as Daniel had expected. Simply to laugh off the Mozart's *Requiem* gambit had left him flailing. No wonder he was painting so keenly.

Harry sat there a few minutes, taking it all in, grinning at the irony of the situation. Then Daniel announced, 'Good,' and turned on the little light over his canvas. He and Harry looked at his work. It could have been a man with very spiky hair and limbs like hose pipes, or a big flower with lots of petals. Or a large number of long, unconnected brush strokes with no particular intent. Harry looked at it, then at Daniel. 'You love her, don't you?' Daniel raised his eyebrows, and chuckled.

That night, Katie and Daniel went to see a movie. It was an American film, about Generation X-ers. It had got fairly good reviews, and lots of magazines had been talking about the Generation X phenomenon – the twenty-somethings who came out of college to find no jobs available

147

and who were the first generation to be poorer than their parents. The film was crap. It was a collection of clever-sounding one-liners, obvious observations on icons and fashions of the nineties, a great soundtrack that waited impatiently to pick up each scene as it floundered, and a story as dull as it was messy. It seemed less a film than a concoction of marketable elements. They stayed to the end to see if it got any better, and because Daniel wanted to see who the song over the gas station scene was by.

Katie hadn't been to the cinema in a year, and this film seemed to justify her absence. They ate burgers, fries and malts at a nearby American diner. As Daniel wiped away the last of the ketchup around his mouth, Katie told him that Mozart's *Requiem* was one of her favourite pieces of music too. He nodded and grinned and let her savour her moment of superiority.

They fell into bed. It was late, and they'd both overdone it with the chips, so he brought a large glass of iced water to bed as they were both very thirsty. Nevertheless, when she found him putting the blindfold on her, she didn't resist. Far from it.

Katie got up at about two, parched, and when she padded back with a fresh glass of water, she felt better, her stomach had settled, and she lustily leaned over and began caressing Daniel's back. He emitted occasional groans of pleasure.

'Someone's having fun,' she said, as she tapped into the dream he was having . . .

. . . The light was blue, rather like the blue in Harry's Therapy Room, and yet in the background were candles, hundreds and hundreds of them, twinkling like the night sky. A transparent drape blew in the wind as Daniel felt his whole being entwining with

148

her body. He sensed a leg, and then another, floating in mid-air, his or hers, he didn't know, conscious only of his passion . . .

Katie leaned in closer and stroked all the way down his back as she licked his neck.

. . . Daniel's shoulders rose slowly, majestically, as he felt his midriff grinding triumphantly into female flesh. Hands grabbed his face and pulled it down to a pair of wet, demanding lips. His own hands snaked along a leg, slowly twisting with desire as her hips undulated with pure lust. He grabbed her ankle and squeezed as she squeezed his manhood . . .

Katie moved on top of Daniel and gasped as she kneaded his elbows and shoulder blades and kissed his back.

. . . Still connected in the most profound and intimate way, Daniel lightly lifted the feminine shoulders that lay beneath him. Willingly, she rose with him, and brought her mouth to his. Caroline's face was racked with ecstasy . . .

CAROLINE! Katie screamed and leapt out of bed.
'Wassup? Whazzit?' asked a bemused Daniel, far from awake, urgently trying to gather his wits.
Katie was getting dressed. 'Take me home!' she screeched.
'Why? What happened?'
'Don't come near me. You're disgusting. You're perverted.'
What was she talking about? The inventive uses to which he'd put an ice cube that night?

'You enjoyed it at the time!' She screamed again. 'Will you stop doing that?'

'Take me home. Now,' she demanded.

'OK, OK, for chrissakes. I'll take you home.' He fumbled his way out of bed.

'No!' She couldn't bear to be with him for a moment longer. 'Call me a cab!'

'It's all right, I'll take you.' He was beginning to think that maybe this was the delayed reaction to Mozart's *Requiem*. He grabbed his jeans, as Katie's rant continued.

'You need to see a psychiatrist.'

'Me?' he questioned, weakly trying to fight back.

But her onslaught went on, unabated, 'You don't even know, do you?'

Daniel was as confused as he was sleepy. As he did up his jeans, she spelt it out for him. 'You were sleeping with Caroline. In your dream.' She pulled on her cardigan and stamped off, in search of her shoes and socks, giving Daniel a moment to think. Caroline? Sleeping with her in his dream? Really?

'Nonsense,' he shouted, not entirely sure of anything.

'You were,' she assured him as she rammed on a sock.

'Look, I was not.' He decided outright denial seemed the best course. Then, as he tried to lift on a sock, he countered, 'Anyway, who said you could read my dreams?' Good point, he thought.

'I didn't know I needed written permission.' On went her right shoe.

He had no proof that he wasn't dreaming about Caroline; he even had a dim recollection. Why would Katie make it up? She wouldn't. He changed tack. 'Look, I just don't remember. But if I did have one I'm sure it wouldn't have been about Caroline, but if it had been about Caroline, then I'm sure that I wouldn't have been sleeping with her.'

150

Katie grunted, her shoelaces tied, and jumped up. 'Just take me home.'

They didn't speak as they walked to the car. It was raining. Very hard. Katie stared straight ahead as Daniel drove. He used the silence to consider it all. So what if he had been dreaming about Caroline? He couldn't control what he dreamt about, it didn't mean he wanted to really sleep with Caroline? He'd had the weirdest dreams, none of which meant anything. The other night he'd dreamt he was on stage at the Royal Albert Hall with his cleaning lady. She was naked apart from a tartan golfing hat and a paintball splatter gun. Daniel wore a pair of goggles and nothing else. Curiously, when she fired the gun, low-fat mango and nectarine yogurt came out, which she then proceeded to lick off his chest, cheered on by the excited crowd of librarians in the stalls. Had Katie 'seen' that dream? No. Good job, he didn't know what she would think of that, but the point was, dreams didn't mean anything. Or at least these two didn't. Daniel often dreamt of flying, like a bird, and had contented himself that this meant he was fulfilled, or ambitious, or happy with himself, or something good.

He decided to speak. 'And even if I was dreaming about having sex with Caroline . . . So? I mean it was just normal sex? Wasn't it?' He'd suddenly had a horrible thought that perhaps his cleaning lady had been there as well.

Katie ignored him. The point was that he didn't want to have an affair with Caroline. It was Katie he loved. Loved? Yes. Had she read that thought? 'And anyway, I can't remember,' he said.

She just kept looking out of the window. He wanted to know if she was taking this as seriously as she pretended. Surely a dream couldn't mean it was over. 'Is this it then?' he asked calmly.

151

'I don't know.' Daniel concentrated on the road. She looked at him, and added sadly, 'I don't want to wear a blindfold all my life.'

Daniel's heart sank. She was the one who'd said 'Don't be silly' when he'd played Mozart's *Requiem*. What did she want – an automaton as a boyfriend? Or someone who could read her thoughts? But what must it be like for her to read his thoughts? She could see how much he cared for her, but could she see all the other little things: 'I wish she wouldn't do that with the vinegar,' 'Mmm, look at that waitress,' 'I'm knackered,' 'Why has she done her hair like that?' It must be hard. It must make her very insecure. Perhaps she feared giving herself to him too much – but maybe that was exactly what she needed to do. And he needed to show her how much she meant to him, that he really wanted her to be part of his life.

He pulled up outside her flat. They sat in silence for a few moments. Then Katie opened the door, looked at him and said, 'Maybe.' Daniel watched her go inside. Maybe? Maybe what? What was she talking about? He started up the car. Was it something he had been thinking? And her answer was 'maybe'. What had he been thinking? He drove off. He'd got about fifty yards when he remembered. Of course.

He spun the car round and headed back. He leapt out of his car into the pouring rain, with no coat to protect him, only a shirt. He bounded up the steps, pressed her buzzer, banged on the door and impatiently shouted her name. He ran back down the steps to get a clear view of her window, and shouted at the top of his voice, 'Will you . . . will you marry me?' There was no movement from the window. So he took a deep breath and bawled, 'Katie, will you marry me?' Soaking wet, having got a mouthful of rain, he gave it one more shot, endangering his vocal cords, 'Will you marry me?'

She appeared, doing up her red silk dressing-gown, and stepped on to the balcony, shouting, 'I told you. Maybe.' And with a big smile she stepped back into the dry of her flat, leaving Daniel elated on the pavement. He got back into his car. He didn't care that he squelched into the seat, or that his calves were freezing. He put on Roxy Music's 'Love is the Drug', delighted with the situation. Delighted with himself for having put the question – before, he'd flinched at the word 'commitment'; and delighted that she had said yes, well, it was a maybe, but of course that meant yes.

He dashed back home, bounded up to his flat, threw off his soggy clothing, and jumped in the shower. It was four o'clock in the morning, and he just sat in a towel in his living room, watching a pub quiz hosted by that bloke off daytime TV, in which the different teams called themselves things like The Mighty Quins, The Snug Lads, Gertie's Boys, and, incongruously, The Insouciants.

He eventually fell asleep, and then woke up as breakfast TV came on and a man who became a woman then became a man again was being interviewed. The clock in the corner of the screen told him it was 8.03. Not too early to ring people. He rang his parents, his brother, his Uncle Gary, then dialled Harry and Caroline. No, he'd tell Harry in person. He wanted to see his face.

He got dressed, gulped down some coffee and ran down to his car. He wanted to let the traffic cop know the good news. He stopped off at Joe the Florist's, placed an order and bought some flowers, parking on a double yellow line. But she didn't come by. He drove round a bit, badly; over-taking, jumping red lights, but there was no sign of her. In the end he reversed at speed up a one-way street, causing chaos, passing ten cars, evoking hoots from all sides. It did the trick, because he soon heard the siren, and then the motorbike. She pulled in right next to him and Daniel produced a bunch of flowers for her. 'You're a gem,' he told her. She took the flowers with a grin and sniffed them.

In his office, Harry was reading an article about juggling in *The Therapy Journal*, which argued, against the orthodox view that it was good therapy, that this wasn't necessarily so, since the relaxation provided by having to concentrate fully on the activity may be outweighed by the irritation caused by constantly dropping the balls.

Daniel parked his car at the Self Centre and fought his way through a modem of telecommunications experts, heading for a seminar on 'Fibre Optics and Pets – Possible Applications'. He ran up the stairs, along the corridor and burst into Harry's office, breathlessly announcing, 'We're engaged!'

'You what?' asked Harry.

'You heard,' yelled Daniel, bouncing round the office. Harry put down his journal, the news slowly sinking in.

'I don't believe it!' cried Harry, leaping to his feet, needing to see Daniel eye to eye for confirmation. 'When did this all happen?'

'Last night.' They hugged with delight and did a little shimmy.

'Congratulations! That's fantastic!'

Harry was delighted. Never before, in his mind, had marriage and Daniel ever been in the same paragraph, let alone the same sentence. He'd had a slight inkling as with Katie, Daniel had been very different and Harry had sensed that this was what Daniel had been aiming for. But wait a minute. What about Katie? Was it really in the bag? Harry broke away from the hug, and asked gingerly, 'It is definite?'

'I've been on the phone all morning. Course it's definite.' They hugged again.

Joe slowly climbed the ornate steps of the imposing hall of the Natural History Museum, in his hand a single champagne rose. He walked along to Katie's office and knocked on the door. She opened it, and took it with a smile. Joe handed her a card on which was written, 'To my fiancée, from your loving fiancé'. Katie smiled and thanked Joe, and went back into her office, where Sandip was peering through a microscope. He looked at the card as Katie admired the rose. He raised an eyebrow in surprise.

'So, you're engaged?'

'No. I only said maybe.' The single rose was a nice touch, and its significance was not lost on her. Daniel was jumping the gun a little, but she found it endearing.

Sandip sighed, 'We men jump to conclusions too easily. We look for any little sign that we have won our petty battle, and if it comes we hail it as the white flag.' Katie was a little peeved by his condescension.

'Why do you put him down all the time?'

Sandip was taken aback, 'I . . .'

Katie's voice and anger rose, 'He's just an ordinary man.' She put down the rose and walked away from Sandip. 'He may not have your intellectual capacity, he may not be a genius, but he has real emotions. Real feelings. At least he's human.'

Sandip stood still, and looked away from her, showing nothing. He turned away. Katie gulped. She hadn't really meant to be so hard; she just wanted to make Sandip see that Daniel was worth her attention, that she could feel for him and still be a good scientist, something she felt Sandip didn't believe. She wanted to make Sandip respect Daniel, but being nasty to Sandip undermined that, she knew. She moved toward him and tried to conciliate. 'Oh Sandip, I'm sorry.'

Slowly Sandip turned to her, and his voice became

firmer. 'You really disappoint me. Your words have no effect on me. But *you* . . . really disappoint me.' He turned away from her. 'These base emotions destroy my hope for mankind's evolution.'

Katie moved round the bench to him, 'I'm sorry, Sandip, it was just a slip . . .'

'Well, was it?'

She folded her arms and looked at him dolefully. But then she smiled and said, 'It's my turn.'

'What's your turn?' he asked.

Taking her coat, she said, 'To buy lunch. Your stomach's empty.'

He smiled and confirmed, 'So it is.'

Instead of the usual sandwich from the shop round the corner, Katie suggested they go further afield. She wanted to make amends for her nastiness with a slap-up meal. They had no need to rush back for the afternoon. 'Let me take you somewhere special,' she grinned. Sandip had been lent a car by an old friend, the type of ancient Mercedes beloved of dodgy cab drivers the world over. It had done over a hundred thousand miles and still went like a dream, and had that proper smell of old car – genuine leather and wooden dashboard.

They went to Holland Park, picking up take-away sushi at the Hiroko restaurant at the Kensington Hilton just off Shepherd's Bush roundabout. They parked near the Orangery and headed to the Kyoto Gardens, a specially commissioned Japanese garden, a gift from the people of Kyoto, with little waterfalls and ornate chess over carefully planned ponds. Sandip had never been there, and he'd only ever had sushi once. Katie recalled how much he'd loved it, and she thought these the ideal surroundings. He was delighted by his treat, and told her how much he appreciated it, and her work. She knew that, and apologised again as they sat on a bench.

'I don't understand what's happened to you. But it's affecting your work,' said Sandip, as he took some salmon eggs with some chopsticks.

Katie sighed, 'I know.'

Sandip wiped his mouth with a napkin. 'I never thought I'd have to say this –'

Katie interrupted, 'It's all right. You don't need to find someone else.'

There was no way she was going to let him, or herself, down. She'd invested too much in their work together. Sandip eyed her mournfully, 'Staying with the tribe is easier.' Yes. S 1764 G5 had been shunned by hers, and all she'd done was cook her dinner. Most people, including Mrs Dwyer, and Daniel, couldn't understand her passion for work, her simple satisfaction with her life of work, computer Scrabble, computer chess. There was nothing wrong with it, and that was how Sandip lived his life. Yet she knew there was more, and she knew her life with Daniel, or someone, could probably be much more fulfilling, but for the time being she wasn't sure. Only time would show if their relationship was worth making sacrifices for. She'd told Daniel 'maybe'. It was enough that she knew he was serious, though the trip to America still rankled, and she felt 'maybe' was the right answer for the time being. 'Yes' would have to wait, and a 'no' was always a possibility. Take things slowly. See what happens about India.

'I've got my priorities right,' she insisted.

'I'm glad.'

'So when do we find out about the grant?'

Sandip finished his mouthful of salmon eggs, and murmured, 'Today.'

Katie was surprised, 'When?' He said nothing. She looked into his eyes. A little smile cracked his face. 'We got

157

it?' Sandip's smile enlarged. 'Yes! We got it!' screamed Katie, and leapt up, her arms in the air. This was fantastic news. Without the grant, who knows what would have happened to all their research, but now they could see it through. It was only fair, she thought, a just reward for everything she and Sandip had put into it.

Sandip drove them back, with Katie emitting occasional squeaks of jubilation. Sandip smiled, but just as they were parking, reminded her that this would mean she would have to go to India very soon. And tell Daniel. She nodded. It wasn't going to be easy, but this opportunity could not be turned down; she had to see it through. As they walked up the steps to the Natural History Museum, she stopped and gave Sandip a hug. 'Thank you. For everything.' Sandip beamed, and opened the door for her with a bow.

Chapter Ten

As Sandip and Katie entered the lobby an extraordinary sight greeted them. Hundreds of balloons cascaded down from the ceiling, and they heard an organ playing the Wedding March. Lots of people were waiting in the lobby area, all the staff from the museum, Caroline, Harry and several people Katie didn't recognise, probably members of the public and school trips who had been looking round the museum. The music transformed into upbeat dance music and, at the top of the stairs up which Joe had struggled, appeared the shaven head of the lead singer of Right Said Fred, wearing an unbuttoned shiny red jacket and no shirt, intoning the opening lines of a song, 'She's my Mrs, I'll never let her go.'

Katie and Sandip were dumbstruck.

Then the two other members of the group appeared – the second shaven-headed one, playing guitar and wearing an unbuttoned shiny green jacket with no shirt, and a third, blessed with hair, a long black coat and guitar. A spotlight picked them out, and they wandered down the stairs. The lead singer raised his hands aloft and started clapping in time with the beat, a cue taken up by the crowd downstairs, and continued with the song. They reached the landing and the chorus at the same time, where they were joined by Daniel. So that was it. This was all Daniel's idea ... Katie cringed with embarrassment when he pointed at her as they sang, 'She's my Mrs, I'll never let her go.' Daniel showed the lead singer where Katie was, so he could more easily address his sentiments to her. The crowd waved their arms in unison, and Daniel made a gesture of gratitude to the band as he grooved his way down the stairs and bobbed through the crowd, giving Caroline a kiss and Harry a hug on the way.

Breathlessly, he arrived by Katie's side, parting a sea of balloons to reach her as she gave him a deadly look. She was mortified. She'd said maybe, and he had done this, in front of all her workmates, in front of Sandip. Her answer had been far from definite and now she was going to India. Stupid Daniel. She could only guess at how much it had cost him to get the band. Thousands and thousands, probably. A friend of hers had once tried to book Johnny Hates Jazz for a college ball, when they'd been in the charts, and had been horrified at how much they'd quoted. But Daniel didn't care about the cost. He was beside himself with glee.

He kissed her and shouted, 'This place is fantastic. Hi, Sandip.' He looked Katie in the eye and said, 'I guarantee you I've never done this before.'

'Look, Daniel, we need to talk,' she snarled.

'Later, later,' grinned Daniel, letting his legs be seduced by the music.

'No, *now*,' she snapped and yanked him over to a corner. Sandip followed slowly, kicking his way through balloons.

Daniel and Katie went into a corner, leaving the party to continue. 'Don't you think this is all a bit premature?' she rasped.

'Well, I guess we haven't discussed –' Daniel shrugged, still light-hearted.

'Too right we haven't.' Katie took a breath, 'Look, I've been thinking . . .'

'Yes?' asked Daniel, bobbing to the music, unconcerned.

'Well – I mean, I . . . ' faltered Katie.

'You're angry ... Look at your pupils ...'

'Of course I'm fucking angry! I haven't said I'd marry you.' She pushed him away.

'Well, you haven't said you won't,' retorted Daniel. He had been taking his own advice: be confident, assume the answer is yes and it will be.

'Well, I won't.' She'd said it.

'You won't?' said Daniel, closing in on her, knowing how much effort it had taken for her to say that. Could she say it again?

'No, I won't,' she replied, her resolve weakening.

'Why not?' asked Daniel, realising she was serious, now feeling angry and hurt.

'Because she won't,' butted in Sandip.

'What have you got to do with it?' enquired Daniel.

Katie looked at Sandip, letting him take over. 'I know Katie. Don't take it badly. I'm sure there are women who would gladly fall for all this nonsense.' Daniel looked at Katie, for some sort of rebuttal. None came. Sandip continued, warming to his theme, 'But Katie needs a different kind of stimulation,' he tapped his head, '... in here.' Katie couldn't bear to catch Daniel's eye. She looked at Sandip, then at the ground.

'Besides, Katie is coming to India with me.'

Daniel glared at him, 'India?' He looked at Katie, then back at Sandip, and then snarled, 'You bastard,' and punched Sandip squarely on the jaw, sending him flying. Katie rushed over to him, while Daniel tried to deal with the pain in his fist. Punching someone wasn't as easy as he thought.

'Are you OK?' asked Katie, helping Sandip up.

'Of course, I was expecting this,' said Sandip, ever the anthropologist. Daniel found it incredibly irritating, and Sandip continued in similar manner, 'A perfectly natural knee-jerk reaction. The aggressive fist attack has been the same across the animal kingdom for millennia. Pride.'

Daniel was preparing his fist as Sandip advanced, but Sandip's only weapon was theory, 'A second attack, however, would be illogical . . . unless, of course, there is more than a bruised ego at stake.'

Katie looked at Daniel. It was a moment of choice for both of them. Daniel's eyes darted between Sandip and Katie, but her cold eyes gave him no comfort. He had been outflanked and felt very weak. Sandip pressed home his advantage, 'Don't deceive yourself with feelings. It's thoughts that count.' Daniel glanced once more at Katie, then turned his back and left, leaving Katie drained, with a sick feeling in her stomach. She gave Sandip a reassuring smile: he had saved her from a terrible mistake.

Daniel ran out through a sea of balloons as Right Said Fred continued their song.

He was angry. He was sad. He was bitter. Perhaps Sandip was right. She really only cared about her work. Deep down, maybe he'd always be just a bullshit psychologist to her. On his way home he called the Self Centre and cancelled his afternoon seminar. He didn't have the heart. He spent an hour watching children's television. Then he had a shower. He looked at the bed. The sheets smelt of her; not just her perfume, but something indefinably her. He took them off the bed and to the bathroom and put them in the laundry basket. Her toothbrush caught his eye. He snatched it and threw it in the bin, along with all her bits and bobs.

That night Harry called, but Daniel didn't pick up the phone; he let the answering machine do it. Harry's message was one of congratulations, but mystification as to where Daniel had gone. Why had he disappeared from the party? Daniel couldn't bear to tell Harry. He felt stupid.

He ordered in a pizza. A large. He normally only had a medium, but today he ate a large. And garlic bread. He went to bed heavy, and told himself that's why he wasn't sleeping. In the morning his eyes showed what a night he'd had. He put on his sunglasses. On his way to work, he stopped at the lights, and, before he could stop her, the same girl as before was cleaning his windscreen. She gave him a smile, but he wasn't there to return it, he was in India.

Katie stayed late at work that day. There was so much to do before she went away. Work was good. Work was simple. The rose had been thrown away, but a petal had dropped on her bench. Work couldn't prevent a tear, and then another. She was trying to piece together two small fragments of bone, but the tweezers just wouldn't do what she wanted. She went home, made herself some pasta with the remains of some of Mrs Positano's sauce. It would pass. India was where she should be.

She slept fitfully, dreaming of India, but Daniel was there, and so, bizarrely, was the waiter from Angelino's, dancing in a Hawaiian grass skirt. The next morning she woke up early, and as she sat eating her toast nothing made sense. It was probably best to go away now. Finish with Daniel now, any longer would be more painful. After all, he dreamt about Caroline, his best friend's wife. But then, she'd dreamt about the waiter from Angelino's. But Daniel flirted with Caroline. And he was silly to organise that stunt with Right Said Fred at the Museum. Silly. She wished she could see Sandip. He was so wise: he knew her well, and his advice was strong and impartial, but he'd gone to Leeds and Manchester to give some lectures.

She headed off to work. By mid-morning, fed up with not being able to concentrate, she went to Harrods' games department to buy herself a computer backgammon set. That would be good. As she walked back into the museum, the commissionaire gave her a nod and a smile, humming Right Said Fred's song 'Be my Mrs', and dancing a bit. She just smiled in return. There'd been a lot of that, people grinning at her: people she'd realised had thought her rather cold and uptight now obviously looked on her differently since her fiancé had pulled such a stunt. She hadn't told them it was off. She couldn't face it. Let them find out once she'd gone to India.

By mid-afternoon, she felt she'd done enough and could go home. In fact, she was getting nowhere, but it could wait till she got to India. She walked and walked, through Knightsbridge, through Green Park, Piccadilly, and did a bit of window-shopping in Covent Garden. Should she buy some clothes for India? She went to The Gap and picked up three white tee-shirts. That would do.

Then she found herself strangely drawn to the Aldwych. To Mrs Dwyer's office, where Daniel had followed her down in the lift and invited her to Angelino's. Perhaps if he was still as keen as that after her being in India for six months, then she'd know. Yes, whatever happened, going to India was right. If he could wait, and she could, she'd be sure it was something meaningful. But he wouldn't wait: surely, he'd go off with someone; someone who was easily taken in by his body language nonsense, his flowers and his array of tricks. Anyway, he was going to America and he hadn't told her how long for. Maybe he had someone in America, and if he told Katie about the lecture tour, he'd have to tell her about this someone; maybe this someone was serious.

She was standing outside the building. People were rushing home. The red-head that had so embarrassed Daniel came hurrying out. Katie went in and got in the lift. She sat down, and pressed the button. When it reached Mrs Dwyer's floor she sat there, trying to work it out. Most people were gone by now, so there was no call for the lift. She sighed. Perhaps India wasn't the answer. Perhaps she was running away from the best thing that had happened to her, and it wouldn't be there when she came back. Look at Sandip. Did she want to be like that? He seemed quite happy to be married to his work. Was that enough for her?

Her stomach was fluttering with indecision when she heard a door being shut and locked. Footsteps approached the lift. It was Mrs Dwyer. 'Oh, Miss Burrill, hello. Are you all right?'

Katie was flustered. How could she explain her presence there? Any excuse would be transparent, so she opted for boldness and honesty. 'I'm going to India in a couple of days, but I don't know if I'm in love.'

'In love?' Wonders will never cease, thought Mrs Dwyer, having put Katie down as a no-hoper in the love stakes. 'Does he love you?'

'He asked me to marry him.'

'Yes, but you want to know if he'll love you in six months, six years, sixty years?'

Katie looked at Mrs Dwyer, intrigued by her insight, 'Yes.' That was something someone like Sandip never had to consider – work was work, unchanging, controllable. People were different, unpredictable.

'And you want to know if you'll still love him?' continued Mrs Dwyer. Katie looked at her by way of affirmation. Mrs Dwyer sat beside her. 'The answer, Miss Burrill, is that nobody can ever know. You have to decide if it's worth the risk. And it is a risk. Marriage doesn't equal security. Quite the opposite. Look at me ... Mr Dwyer died. Nothing prepares you for that. Were our years together worth the awful pain of losing him? What if those years had only been months? What if he had been unfaithful? You have to take all this and more on if you marry someone. The easy answer is not to marry, but it may not be the right one.'

Mrs Dwyer pressed the button for the ground floor. She gave Katie a little hug when they parted outside the building. Katie wandered back home, and that night played with her new computer backgammon, losing four times, unable to concentrate.

Daniel went straight to Harry's office. Harry was in the Therapy Room, painting what looked to Daniel like an exploding peach, but Harry assured him it was entitled 'Autumn'. But Harry could sense straight away that Daniel was not himself.

'Where did you get to yesterday?'

'She said no. We're not getting married. She was angry about the party, then she said it.'

'Hey, Daniel, I'm sorry.'

'Of course, he was there.'

'Who?'

'Lover boy. Sandip. He's a genius. He's taking her to India. He knows what she wants, you see.' Daniel jabbed at his own head. 'Up here, you see, that's where she needs stimulation. Yeah, I know damn well where he'll be giving her stimulation. See, he's told her that a bullshit psychologist is not good enough for her.'

'She's having an affair with him?'

'No! He's asexual, I think. Can only think about his stomach. And bones. And some woman he's found in India.'

'He's having an affair with this woman?'

'No, she's thousands of years old, but he likes her bone structure. She was clever, you see. She didn't run with the pack. Katie thinks she's like her.'

'She's told you this?'

'No, but I felt it. An undercurrent, when she told me a bit about her work. And about Sandip. The genius who picked her up and took her under his wing. She told me about the grant, but I didn't know it meant going to India. She didn't tell me she was about to piss off to India with Genius-Features.'

'You didn't tell her you *weren't* about to piss off to America.'

'Yeah.'

'How long is she going to India?'

'I don't care. For ever, as far as I'm concerned.'

'You could visit her . . . she might come back in a few months . . . it's a good chance to see if you really love her.'

'You idiot! She turned me down! She said no! Sandip's had his . . . intellectual way with her. I couldn't stand ever to see her again!'

'Do you love her?'

'Of course!'

'Go and see her.'

'No! Anyway, I've got work to do.' And Daniel strode out of the Therapy Room, out of Harry's office and along the corridor, and headed off to berate some businessmen on the finer points of communication.

Harry sat alone. He had wondered if Daniel hadn't jumped the gun. It was all very sudden. Katie had seemed very unsure at the swimming pool. Her natural reaction seemed to be circumspection. Agreeing to marry Daniel so quickly didn't seem to be her style. And what about this Sandip? What were his motives? Was it that he didn't want to lose a valuable colleague?

Harry and Daniel had first met at Harry Porter University, West Carolina. Harry was a native of Mendham, New Jersey, a small town within reach of Newark. His father, a realtor, dreamed of sending his bright son to an Ivy League law school, which Harry duly fulfilled before dropping out at the beginning of his final year, leaving to go in search of something more meaningful in the Far East.

He travelled through Thailand, India, the Kingdom of Bhutan, and, after nine months, ended up on the Indonesian island of Bali. He settled in Ubud, in the mountains, a town which had long been a refuge for writers and artists. He spent six months there, learning to paint and to carve wood in the traditional local style. He enjoyed being one of the cognoscenti, able to observe with detachment the Europeans who came through, those on package tours, and the backpackers on their way to the hilltop Hindu temples or the nearby monkey forest.

Eventually, he decided it was time to leave, so he caught a boat to Darwin in northern Australia, a real frontier town that had been all but destroyed in a 1974 cyclone, and which still struggled to resolve the conflicts between its Asian climate, its Aboriginal background, and the Europeanness of its would-be conquerors. Harry loved it, and stayed six months, working for the Northern Territory Arts Association, which brought culture from all over Australia and the world. Often he would drive entertainers down the highway, in places no more than a dirt track to points south, to Alice Springs. They would stop at villages, and perform for no more than a handful of people who would marvel at the shows given by dancers, jugglers, actors or magicians.

Harry loved the Aborigine nation's notion of 'walkabout', the seemingly unpredictable period spent wandering in the bush, which could occur at any time, and last as long as it took. Eventually, he felt that his own walkabout was over, and that it was time to return to America.

He headed back to the States, and enrolled in the

American studies course at West Carolina. It was something of a disappointment, mainly because of the standard
of the other students. When asked in a lecture what the In-
cas traded in, and given a clue that it had something to do
with olives (the answer being olive oil), one student said,
'Was it pizza?' perfectly seriously. Harry felt he may have
made a mistake, and spent much of his time shooting pool
and watching baseball with Daniel, who was there doing a
one-year postgraduate course in non-verbal communication.

When Daniel returned to England, Harry, ever keen to
travel and to see Europe, came with him. Once he'd met
Caroline, his fate was sealed. Her family was fairly well
off, and she had an administrative job with a travel firm, so
she was able to support him while he got his formal training as an art therapist.

Harry had never known Daniel to make such a
misjudgment. He simply didn't get hurt by relationships,
always managing them so as to minimise heartache. But
not this time. Harry didn't know what to do – start a
damage limitation exercise along the lines of 'she just
wasn't for you', or encourage Daniel to fight on, a possibly
useless rearguard action.

In Daniel's lectures that day, the words came out, the
little gimmicks and showmanship, but he didn't care. At
the end of the day, he just sat in Harry's Therapy Room,
staring into space. Harry knew him well enough not to
interrupt. He'd offered him dinner, or a bed for the night,
but Daniel declined. Eventually Daniel stood up and said
goodbye. Harry wondered if it would help were Caroline
to go and see Katie. 'No,' Daniel snapped. Harry offered to
go himself. Daniel shrugged, and murmured, 'See you
tomorrow,' before leaving.

When Daniel got home, he looked round his flat mourn-fully. He stood on the coffee table, and took it all in – the fireplace in front of which they'd made love, the draw-bridge sofa, the flowers she'd brought him last week, the other sofa where Sandip had sat as Daniel surveyed his body language, the window out of which he'd looked when she'd said, 'Don't be silly.' Who was being silly now? Why had she broken it off? What had Sandip been up to? Did he fancy her, after all? Daniel's fist still hurt from punching him, but he didn't regret it. So what if it was animal behaviour: he wanted to win the female, and San-dip was his rival – or was her work the rival? Did she have to go to India, or was she running away because she didn't love him, or because she feared he wasn't committed? But he was committed . . . he'd never asked anyone to marry him before. He'd certainly never spent several grand getting a bald man to sing 'She's my Mrs' to someone before.

He went into the bathroom and fished out the sheets from the laundry basket. They still had her musk about them. The smell thrilled him. He looked in the bin, and fished her toothbrush out. There must be a way: maybe he should send Harry round. Harry's unconniving nature, his honest approach and genuine feeling for Daniel, might win her over. He went to the kitchen and ripped down the 'US lecture tour' post-it note. He still had the sheets in his hand as he wandered to the bedroom and lay down with the sheets pressed close to him. He was exhausted. He'd had very little sleep the night before, thinking, day-dreaming, half-sleeping, dreaming – about Sandip, the punch, the colonnades on Hampstead Heath, and the wreath she'd sent him. Life seemed very grim. He'd lost Katie. Was he going to end up a sad old bachelor, still playing games when he was sixty? He didn't wake till the next morning.

Katie was up bright and early. She got out a couple of suit-cases, and put a few things on her bed, ready for packing. Then she decided to treat herself to a trip to Waterstones to buy some books for the trip. She was browsing through the shelves, looking at the history section, when she realised a man near her was looking at her. He was middle-aged, with a grey jacket, dark tie and astronaut hair, and he was thinking, 'Tasty, very tasty.' She glared at him and moved off to a nearby shelf of oversize books. She'd just caught sight of *Great Moped Journeys of the World* when she be-came aware of being looked at again and thought about by a tall man with beard and glasses, who mused, 'Great legs.' She sidled around the end of the shelf, brushing past a shorter man with a sports jacket and greying temples. She could tell what was in his mind: 'Nice perfume.' She headed to another section, aware that another man, in a smart dark suit, eagerly leafing through a book on the state of the arts, was thinking, 'What a mouth.' She turned in another direction, where a dissolute figure in stripy bermuda shorts with a cigarette behind his ear looked at her, and thought, 'Some figure.'

She crossed her arms in fury, and looked at them all, sur-rounding her with their intrusive thoughts. A tear welled up in her eye, and she screamed, 'The lot of you can just fuck off, OK?' Another tear appeared and she looked down and covered her face. The men stared at her, and slowly began to drift away.

A young assistant wandered over to see what the com-motion was. 'Madam, please –' but she was gone. She went to work and tidied her desk, thinking about India. She went to bed very early, and contented herself with playing simultaneous games of computer backgammon, chess and Scrabble, and fell asleep in a losing position in all three.

Daniel was being entertained by Harry and Caroline. He'd

put little Clare to bed, and had then drunk far too much wine over dinner. His hosts kept giving each other little looks; this wasn't like Daniel, but Harry saw him get this way once every couple of years. Perhaps he needed to. When it was time to go home, they insisted he stay in the spare bedroom, to which he readily agreed, bidding them goodnight by telling them how much he loved them, then returning a couple of minutes later in his underpants to repeat this sentiment, but adding that he loved Katie most of all.

Over a cup of herbal tea, Caroline and Harry discussed what they should do. Harry decided that he should see Katie. He and Daniel had talked about it, and he had to do something. He hated seeing his best friend being reduced to a lovesick drunk. The next morning, as with a slightly heavy head Daniel gave Clare her breakfast, Harry explained what he would try and say to Katie. Daniel didn't know if it was a good plan or not. Part of him was too proud, and thought she should come to him, but he wanted her back. Harry proposed total honesty. Daniel knew this was the best plan. Harry would tell her what Daniel was going through, how he really felt, and about the phantom American trip. It wouldn't be easy, and Daniel was going to have to work very hard at any follow-up, but it had to be done.

Harry ate a hearty breakfast. He wasn't looking forward to it. Katie was rather scary, and not just because of her ESP, although that certainly unnerved him. Caroline and Daniel waited while he went on his mission.

Chapter Eleven

That morning Katie showered and threw on her red silk dressing-gown before attacking the suitcases again. What to pack? It was daunting. She'd been to India once before, but that was only for a month.

Her front-door buzzer went. And again. She pressed the entry button. Was it Daniel? She turned and walked back to continue packing. As the door opened, she zipped up the case and turned. It was Harry. 'Hi,' he said gingerly. 'Can I come in?'

So, Daniel had sent his friend. Too lily-livered to come himself. 'OK, let's hear it. I've got a plane to catch.' She sat in an armchair, impatiently.

Harry tried to find the right words, then said simply, 'Daniel sent me.'

'I knew that,' she snapped.

'Right,' said Harry, his confidence draining, but he continued. 'I'll get straight to the point then. He's not going to the States. He never was. Just another game.'

She crossed her arms, 'Typical.'

Harry took a big breath, and explained, 'Yeah, well, he knows it was a big mistake, and now . . . now he really just . . . he desperately wants –'

'– To marry me. Anything else?' she butted in, unmoved and unimpressed, which made Harry angry.

'You know, you are quite something,' he said. 'Personally I think he's mad. Living –'

'– With me would be quite insufferable. Ho hum.' Harry

was aware he wasn't winning this, but irritation made him want to speak his mind.

'You know you should really take a look at yourself. Danny is . . . well, he's the best friend I've ever had. He's –'

'– Loyal, he's funny, he's charming . . .'

'Right,' he was getting angry, 'and you should feel lucky –' She looked away in high-handed disdain. '– Yes, lucky!' he shouted, wanting to make her see sense, '– that he's willing to put up with all this ESP crap. He loves you. He can't stop thinking about you.'

She snarled bitterly, 'Oh yes he can,' and wandered to the window.

Out of her gaze for a few moments, Harry regained his cool. He stepped towards her, conciliatory again. 'He cares about you. This is the first time. You are the only one. Of course he makes mistakes. He's confused. We all are. We can't replace our minds with computers.'

Katie looked him in the eye. 'I'd appreciate it if you'd stop thinking about what I'm wearing under this while you try to reason with me.'

Harry was horrified and bewildered, 'Excuse me?'

She was very matter of fact, 'You heard me.'

'I was not,' he insisted.

'Oh, you weren't?' she moved away from the window, and leant against the fireplace,

'Like you weren't thinking about me in the car when I said you were tired and didn't want to eat?' Her eyes locked on his. 'Nothing,' she taunted him, 'I'm wearing *nothing* underneath. Do go on.'

Harry took a breath. The attack had left him weakened. OK, maybe she was right about the incident in the car, but that was Clare's fault for mentioning her bosoms. Calmly he told her, 'You know, I love Caroline. I think strange things about stranger people. But I still love Caroline.'

She folded her arms, and spoke defiantly, 'I suppose I shouldn't be surprised that you should be so alike. Maybe if we got married we could have wife-swapping parties.'

His eyes narrowed suspiciously, 'What's that supposed to mean?'

There was no stopping Katie now, 'He's your friend. Your . . . *loyal* friend. How is Caroline?'

Harry couldn't believe what he was hearing. 'You are a real bitch,' he said, and walked away from her, unable to look her in the eye.

She shouted after him, 'Look, I'm trying to help you. I'm trying to show you the real Daniel Becker.'

Harry put his hands to his ears, 'No. You can screw up your own life, but I won't listen to this.' He headed to the door.

She screamed, 'You haven't heard the half of it.'

He opened the door, 'You know what? I don't give a shit,' and then off he went, down the stairs.

She ran to the window, and bawled down when he came out, 'Well, you should.' Harry opened his car door, intent on ignoring Katie, who continued, 'She's your wife!' Harry gave her a dirty look and drove off.

Daniel and Caroline were waiting. Caroline reclined on the sofa, sewing back the arm of Clare's cuddly rabbit, while Daniel paced up and down, bouncing a basketball. They heard the front door open, and in came Harry. Daniel pounced. Harry sat in an armchair, having thought long and hard on his drive back. Daniel sat facing him, on the coffee table.

Daniel leapt in with, 'How did it go? What did she say?'

Harry took a breath, his stomach churning, 'She's leaving in the morning.'

'No, Harry, she can't, she just can't!' Daniel was bitterly disappointed. He'd thought Harry's straightforward

175

approach would bring dividends, but now he'd have to go himself. He got up and began pacing and bouncing the ball again.

Harry gathered himself. 'Daniel, I have one question for you.'

'Yeah, shoot,' murmured Daniel, his mind on the next tactic to stop Katie going away.

'Are you fooling with my wife?'

This stopped Daniel abruptly. He grabbed the basketball and turned to Harry. 'No! Did she say that?'

'In as many words, yeah.'

Caroline laughed it off, 'That's ridiculous.'

'Oh, is it?' Harry had tried hard to work out how it could possibly be true, and had found no evidence, but still he had to be sure.

They both looked at Daniel for some sort of explanation. 'For chrissakes, it was a dream,' he began pacing and bouncing again.

'About me?' asked Caroline, with a chuckle.

'Yeah,' replied Daniel. 'You know, about you.'

'Was it good?' enquired Caroline, intrigued.

'What sort of dream?' bawled Harry, butting in, looking daggers at his wife for her frivolous line of enquiry.

Daniel, feigning innocence, muttered, 'You know . . . I don't know, I can't remember. Caroline, would you talk to her, you know, woman to –'

Harry erupted, leaping to his feet and pushing Daniel to the wall, demanding, 'You have dreams about my wife?'

Daniel was desperate, 'Yeah, well, I wouldn't dream about her if she didn't flirt with me.'

'I beg your pardon?' said Caroline, rising to her feet. Now she was angry.

Harry looked at her, then at Daniel, and disdainfully released him, snarling, 'Get out.'

Caroline pointed to the door, 'I think you'd better go.'

'Yeah, me too,' agreed Daniel, and left.

He drove home slowly, disconsolately. He put on the car stereo. 'Love is the Drug'. He switched to the radio. Someone had requested 'We Don't Talk Any More' by Cliff Richard for their girlfriend. He found another station. A talk station, where a Conservative MP was saying what a good idea it was that so many national utilities had been privatised, and that he saw nothing wrong with these privatised companies then making donations to the Conservative Party, and putting former ministers, who oversaw the privatisations, on to their boards, nor with executives making massive profits from share options. Daniel turned it off.

He sat alone in his flat. Miserable. He couldn't imagine what could make him more miserable. He'd lost his girlfriend – his fiancée – and his best friends. Harry and Caroline would probably come round in the end. But . . .

He had the lights off. He wanted the darkness to reflect that of his soul. He doodled on a pad. He'd read all the magazines he had, even the articles you don't read till you've read all the ones you want to read. The doodles might help him, he thought. Sometimes he had found Harry's art room therapeutic, so why not try a bit of his own? However, looking at what he came up with provided no clue as to what to do next. There were just lots of circular, concentric lines, spiralling to nowhere.

The door buzzer went. Someone at the front door. He put the pad in his pocket and got up. Was it Katie? Had her feelings got the better of her? His heart sunk when he saw it was the female cop. She offered him a spare helmet, and coolly told him, 'Just do it.' She meant business, so he followed her down the stairs and got on to the back of her motorbike. There was an emergency that had to be dealt

177

with. And Daniel could help. Daniel could hardly know what was awaiting him.

A crazed gunman had asked for him by name. A crazed gunman named Parris.

Since Parris had walked out of Daniel's seminar and gone to Harry for some therapeutic art, his life had been turned upside down. When Harry had gone into the Therapy Room half an hour after Daniel had put his head round the door, he found Parris sitting relaxing, admiring his painting of a Colt .45. Harry had not 'judged', as was his practice – he just wanted his clients to express themselves fully and freely, and whatever came out was 'right'. This, Harry assumed, was Parris's reaction to Daniel's control theories, and his gun, both metaphorical and real. He said goodbye to Parris, who had shaken him firmly by the hand, and looked him straight in the eye, with an intense 'goodbye'. There had been a glint, like the one that had unnerved Bob Narley, in Parris's eye which took Harry aback somewhat. But he'd cheerily wished Parris good luck nevertheless.

Parris strolled out of the Self Centre a man of conviction. He was ready to assert himself, to take control, to grab this beast called life and give it all the chutzpah he could muster. He headed for the library where he worked and went straight to Mr Sharples's office, and knocked firmly. Sharples, a balding, grey-haired, grey-suited, middle-aged man in glasses, who had given his working life to libraries and librarians, and had risen steadily in his career, rarely got visitors.

'Come in,' he said, with a slight question in his voice. Parris firmly opened the door, just as he had learnt, and strode up to Sharples's desk, looking him straight in the eye. Sharples was not used to this. He had not been expecting to see Parris either, who was supposed to be away for the week, presumably on holiday. Sharples gave him an avuncular smile. Parris was having none of it.

To Sharples, Parris was loyal and would make a head librarian one day, but he had much to learn. To Parris, Sharples was what stood between him and success. Sharples may have the big desk and the office with his name on the door, but Parris had chutzpah, and a 'gun'. He had a metaphorical gun in his pocket at all times now. Even Julie had noticed.

'Good morning. I've come to talk to you about promotion. My promotion. It's overdue.'

Sharples was a little surprised, and had been preparing for a discussion of holidays, and that it was always nice to get home, wasn't it. Promotion was not on his agenda. There was no vacancy in this library. There were already two senior librarians, and Parris would have to wait his turn, or seek advancement elsewhere. Parris would get there one day, but the claims of Miss Steen and Mr Sweeney had been stronger, and he made no apology for it.

'Sit down, Mr Parris . . . Ian.' Sharples was ready to offer tea, but Parris was not ready to drink it.

Parris looked him straight in the eye. 'I'll stand.'

'Tea?' offered Sharples.

'No tea.' Parris's stare was unnerving Sharples, who also couldn't quite understand why Parris kept his right hand in his pocket all the time.

'Well, then, umm –'

'My promotion. That's what I want, Sharples.'

'Yes, that's all very well, umm, Ian, but –'

'No ifs, no buts, Sharples. I've got ambitions. Big ambitions. Yes, even beyond Deputy Head Librarian. I'm going places.' Sharples was stunned. He couldn't work out which was more bewildering – what Parris was saying, or the way his hand was twitching in his pocket. What was in there?

179

Sharples wondered what Parris had been doing with his holiday.

'Ian, perhaps you need a few extra days off . . . please, help yourself.'

'I've got a few things to sort out at home,' snarled Parris on his way out. Sharples breathed a sigh of relief. 'But I'll be back.' And with that he slammed the door behind him, and headed out through the library. He passed Miss Steen, who offered a smile, but Parris strode on regardless, leaving her to raise an eyebrow of surprise.

He went home, jostling a man on the tube who had inadvertently elbowed him. The man – it was Nigel Johnson in fact, trying to read *Woman's Gazette*, which had an article about a woman who hadn't had sex for forty years – moved away, and Parris felt strong. When a seat became available, a teenager looked at it, moved toward it, but Parris caught his eye, and the teenager let him have the seat. A busker with a guitar came along the carriage, and sang 'Yesterday' badly for his captive audience. A few generous souls put money in his hat, but not Parris, who reprimanded him severely. Looking at the coins in the hat, Parris said, 'I see, and what proportion of this will be going to the publisher of that Lennon–McCartney song? Can I take it as read that the Performing Rights Society –'

The busker got off at the next stop.

Parris did some gardening at home. Some weeding, and also getting rid of plants that were taking over too much of the beds. He yanked out five bin-bags' worth of flora. When Julie came home she was shocked by the denuded garden and wondered if perhaps her husband had pulled up some 'good' plants, as well as 'bad' weeds. What had happened to the convolvulus for a start? Parris told her not to concern herself with it, that the garden was neater, stronger, better for his attack, and his life needed similar treatment. He was taking control. Julie wondered what this meant.

It meant, announced Parris, that promotion would soon be his. That he would play squash with Phillip whenever he wanted. That he would eat his dinner in front of *Tomorrow's World* without interruption. That he would cook dinner every Thursday and it would be lamb chops and Julie would have to eat them. That they would have sex on Mondays, Wednesdays, and Saturdays, with Fridays and Sundays being optional, but at least three of one or the other per month. And that the slippers which he liked so much, and which he had told Julie he had thrown away, would be retrieved from the shed, and worn as and when he pleased.

Julie took this all in. Wednesdays had tended to be his squash nights of late, and he'd got cramp more than once after a session, just putting his feet on the coffee table, so she feared that sex might entail a physiotherapist to be on hand, but she said nothing. Parris was not in a mood to be contradicted. There was something in his eyes, and he kept putting his hand in his pocket when he wanted to make a particular point strongly. 'Yes, Ian,' was her response.

'Good.'

They passed a weekend with Julie having to submit to increasing tyranny. At the supermarket when she put streaky bacon in the trolley he pointed out that he had never liked it and had always preferred back bacon. He insisted on driving, telling her that she was far too timid behind the wheel, and lacking in anticipation. At home he announced that he didn't want all her bills and papers left sprawling over the coffee table, and that she would have to tidy them up, and keep them that way.

She was only too relieved when they left for work on Monday morning. He had bought some sparkling wine, and put it in the fridge in anticipation of his impending promotion, which he was sure would occur that day. Julie wondered if promotion was likely so soon, and was beginning to feel some regret about sending him out to be more self-assertive.

Parris made his way to work as usual, telling a man on the tube to turn down his Walkman so that Parris wouldn't have to put up with the insistent tinny beat of Chaka Demus and Pliers refracted through the listener's head. He demanded that a man who was reading Parris's paper over his shoulder had to give him half the cover price for the privilege. By the time he got to work, he was well primed for the showdown with Sharples. When Sharples saw Parris entering, he hid in Philosophy. He hoped Parris had calmed down. But when he heard Parris ordering Mr Sweeney to make him coffee, he feared the worst.

After three days of behaving with his colleagues and his wife as if he were Head Librarian, or more, Sharples had not given him the expected promotion, but merely enquired whether perhaps he should go home and have a lie down. Parris's patience finally wore out and he found that the metaphorical gun in his pocket was insufficient. He would have to get a real one. Then they'd understand. Then he'd get enough respect.

He sought out a pub in the East End which he'd read about in an article describing how easy it was to get a gun in nineties' London. The Lamb and Mint Sauce was near Mile End station. Parris had told Julie he was working late in Reference, that she could see one of her friends till about nine o'clock, but he still expected his conjugal rights, it being a Wednesday. Parris peered at his street map to get his bearings. He felt a little uneasy, but sought comfort in the imaginary gun in his pocket, knowing that soon it would be a real one.

He found the pub, and ordered a pint of the most dange-
rous-looking beer. He sipped it slowly sitting on a bar
stool, letting the regulars get a good look at him. He engaged the landlord in conversation, dropping his aitches
where possible, complimenting him on the beer, which
actually tasted like industrial drain cleaner mixed with
treacle, with a dash of brown colouring and gas. They
moved on to the weather, and West Ham's prospects. Parris did as best he could, trying to say 'ain't' as much as
possible, to sound more authentic, but unsure of where to
put it in the sentence. Soon though, Parris jumped in with
the real reason for his visit.

'I want a shooter. And I'm willing to pay. I've got several
monkeys and a pony, if you can see me right.' Parris wasn't
sure what monkeys and ponies were – he thought one was
a hunded pounds and the other fifty, but didn't know
which was which.

The landlord looked at him with a frown of suspicion.
'You the filth?'

Parris had been waiting for this, 'Do I look like the filth?
I'm on me own.'

'Yeah, no copper would be stupid enough to come here
on his own.' Parris agreed, saying that you'd have to be
pretty stupid to come here on your own and taking a large
gulp of the industrial drain-cleaner beer, which made him
gag a bit.

This seemed to impress the landlord, who suddenly got
rather edgy and asked, 'Here, you're not workin' for Ron-
nie Ward, are you?'

Parris shook his head. The landlord continued, 'Oo are
you workin' for then?'

'Sharples,' came Parris's swift reply, followed by another
large gulp of beer. It seemed to give him the necessary gravitas and streetwise aplomb. It also made him a bit tipsy,
thus a tad more confident.

'Where's 'e operate then?' The landlord was intrigued by this new name, anxious to stay on the right side of any 'firm'.

'Another manor, umm like,' responded Parris. ''E keeps a low profile.' Another swig, and tipsy gave way to tiddly.

The landlord seemed to be won over. He looked from side to side. 'Come back Monday. I'll see yer right.'

'Splendid,' gleamed Parris. 'How much?' He hoped that the answer would be numerical rather than zoological – he couldn't deal with ponies and monkeys and goats.

'Two fifty, including commission.'

'Two fifty,' affirmed Parris, nodding and draining his glass before gently staggering towards the door.

The cop and Daniel drew up on her motorbike outside the library. There was full police back-up – patrol cars, ambulances, searchlights, SWAT teams, snipers on the roof, and a ginger-haired man with a megaphone. The officer in charge greeted Daniel. They agreed that it was best for him to go in alone, unprotected and unarmed.

Daniel made his way tentatively along the rows of bookshelves. He turned a corner, and there was Parris, sitting on the floor in Medicine in his green anorak, brown corduroys and brown polo neck, holding a lethal-looking pistol to the sweating head of a middle-aged man in a suit. Sharples. Daniel blurted out, 'Parris, what on earth are you doing?'

Parris took a breath. He'd asked for Daniel when the siege began. Daniel and some cheese sandwiches. The sandwiches were a little soggy, but Daniel had got there fairly quickly. Parris took a breath, his nerves at boiling point, and slowly and pointedly explained, 'I'm taking control. Look at this.' He put the gun to Sharples's head. 'Say "hello" to Mr Becker.'

Sharples gave Daniel a pleading look, and, in his best cocktail party voice – well, the best he could manage with a crazed Junior Librarian holding a big gun to his head – said, 'Hello, Mr Becker.'

'Hello,' replied Daniel casually, kneeling down next to Parris, and asking him, 'Are you crazy? Taking your boss hostage?'

'Am I crazy?' blinked Parris. 'Ever since I started your course, my wife and I have argued.' Parris thought back to the good old days, before he encountered Daniel Becker, days when he and Julie would gladly share a cuddle on the sofa every day of the week, when Mr Sweeney, instead of ducking into the toilet whenever he saw Parris, would gladly discuss the golden years of the duodecimal system, before microfiches and VDUs invaded the gentle world of librarianship.

'I became a changed man,' he continued.

'Oh really,' interrupted Daniel.

'She hated it!' snapped Parris. 'Tonight she left.' Parris wondered if he could ever go back to his old life – with no guns in his pocket, real or imaginary, and a wife who loved him for what he was, even if she did think his keenness to do the washing unmanly. He rounded on Daniel, pointing the gun at his nose, 'Why do you teach such *nonsense*?'

'It is not nonsense,' insisted Daniel, suddenly becoming aware of the danger posed by an unbalanced librarian with a shooter and a grudge. He tried to reassure Parris of his own motives, to share in Parris's vulnerability, 'I teach what I practise.' Parris took the gun away.

Parris detected the hint of weakness, and asked, 'Has it worked for you?' Daniel didn't answer. 'Well?' said Parris.

'No,' confirmed Daniel. He finally had to admit it, all his confidently asserted theories had brought him nothing. They both looked at the floor, sharing in a reverie of lost love.

185

Parris sighed, 'And I don't suppose you've got any "games" for getting her back?' Daniel looked at him with genuine warmth. He felt responsible. What could he do to help Parris when he couldn't even help himself?

'No, I've had enough games. Really I have.' They both went back to their own sad thoughts, respectively, of Katie and Julie, and how they may never again be part of their respective lives.

Sharples piped up, 'Perhaps you'd like to continue this little heart to heart somewhere else?'

'Shut up!' snapped Parris, waving the gun wantonly in Sharples's direction.

'Yeah, shut up,' agreed Daniel, and remembered why he was here. Calmly, he addressed Parris, 'You shouldn't have listened to a word I said.'

'Well, I did listen, damn you!' The tension and anger made him blink and hyperventilate a little, but then he hit on an idea which he explained to Daniel, using the gun to emphasise his point, 'So we're going to find her and we're going to tell her it's all your fault.'

'OK, I guess I owe you that,' agreed Daniel as Parris got to his feet. Daniel got up too, and led the way out of Medicine.

Parris followed, then turned back to Sharples, pointing the gun at his balding head, and said, 'See you nine o'clock Monday?' Sharples nodded. 'Good,' said Parris, striding off, a spring in his step. Sharples breathed a sigh of relief.

As they neared the end of a row of bookshelves, they heard Daniel's policewoman friend shout out, 'What's going on?'

Parris gripped the gun, and shouted, 'We coming out.'

'Ian, is that you?'

Parris stepped out from behind the shelves to reveal himself, and shouted, 'Julie?'

She was standing there in her cream overcoat at the end of the aisle with the policewoman, who said, 'She still loves you. Put the gun down.' But Parris wasn't sure whether to believe it. He needed to hear Julie say it.

'Do you? Do you forgive me?' he asked, desperately. 'I won't be aggressive ever again,' he bawled, hoping to persuade her.

'I forgive you. I came out looking for you.' She didn't want him to do anything stupid, she wanted him to put down the gun, but most of all, she wanted her old Ian back. But her husband still needed convincing.

'You promise?'

'I promise,' she replied, her heart pounding and her fingers knotting themselves in tension.

Parris was convinced, almost. One thing would make him certain. 'You'll let me do the ironing?' This was a lot to ask. Julie paused. But she wanted him back, almost at any price.

'Yes, all right,' she screamed, mentally and physically drained.

The cop was getting a little impatient, 'We're all very happy for the two of you. Now can you put the gun away?' Parris looked at Daniel, who nodded, then he ran forwards towards his charging wife, her arms open ready to embrace him. They hugged and kissed in a frenzy of emotion. Parris still had the gun as he held Julie tight, but the policewoman calmly plucked it from him on her way down the aisle towards Daniel, who had got out his doodling pad.

'How did you know where I was?' asked Parris, breathlessly, looking his Love in the eye.

Overcome with relief and happiness, she squeaked, 'I just knew,' and they hugged again.

'What's that?' asked the cop, peering at Daniel's latest doodle, a mess of scribbles much like his earlier effort.

'I think it's me,' said Daniel, pleased to have helped these two lovers together again, but all the more pained by the reminder of his own loss.

'D'you think it or do you know it?' she asked.

'I know it.'

'Right,' she said shutting the book for him, and handing over the gun to a colleague. She led him to her motorbike. Giving him a helmet, she told him they were off to Katie's. He was pessimistic and couldn't see the point, but she insisted. They zipped through London, siren and blue light expediting their journey.

She pulled up outside Katie's house, which the cop remembered from before. Daniel dismounted and thanked her. She wished him good luck and drove off. He ran up the steps, removed his helmet, and pressed her buzzer, once, twice and again, with increasing agitation. Another sturdy press yielded no answer, so he ran down to the pavement and shouted up to her window, 'Katie!' Nothing. There were no lights in her window, and nothing stirred. 'Katie!' he screamed. 'Ka-a-tie!!' at the top of his voice.

A light came on in the flat above Katie's, and a young man peered out, obviously woken by Daniel. Russell Chandler had lived above Katie for a couple of years now, and they occasionally invited one another over for coffee, but otherwise she lived unremarkably. She was quiet, and kept herself to herself, as they say when people have been discovered not keeping themselves to themselves, but in her case it was true, and to have some attractive young man bawling her name in the street late at night was not something Russell would ever have expected. He and Charles had only just nodded off, and didn't need this interruption.

'We're trying to sleep,' exclaimed Russell, fumbling with

188

his glasses. Daniel ignored him, and shouted her name again, even louder.

Then Charles appeared at the window. He'd had time to put on his dressing-gown, and, as Russell managed to get his glasses on straight, told him, 'Tell him we'll call the police.'

Russell nodded, and shouted down, 'We'll call the police,' thinking this might see off this late-night Romeo.

'I am the police!' screeched Daniel, holding up his helmet by way of explanation. Russell and Charles hurriedly retreated back into their flat, shutting the curtains behind them, leaving Daniel to shout her name wildly and vainly one more time.

Chapter Twelve

As a farewell to London, Katie had taken Sandip to Hampstead Heath. She looked up at the full moon, the same moon she would soon be looking at from thousands of miles away. She wandered through the pillars, and smiled, remembering the time she had spent here with Daniel. Sandip was several steps behind, carrying a bottle of champagne and a couple of glasses. 'What is this place?' he asked.

'I discovered it,' she said, then corrected herself sadly, 'we discovered it.'

'We?' asked Sandip, struggling through a bush.

'Daniel,' she murmured as Sandip approached her.

He smiled and said, 'Tonight, let bygones be bygones.' He held out a glass for her, put the other on the floor and took the seal off the champagne. He continued, 'Tonight we should celebrate the success of our work. Fifty thousand pounds,' and popped the cork.

'To ... the future,' toasted Sandip.

'To the future,' echoed Katie, melancholy about the past, and a tear welled up in her eye. She took a sip.

'What is it?' asked Sandip. She sighed.

'I don't know ... I ... I just suddenly felt sad.' His sadness. She looked all around her, not wanting to catch Sandip's searching gaze. 'As though he's just realised that it's all over. Just now.'

She shook her head and took a large swig of champagne, trying to pull herself together. 'I'm sorry. Silly feelings.'

Sandip refilled their glasses, and she held hers to his, and proposed the toast, 'To us. A great team.'

'To us,' repeated Sandip and they clinked.

They were not alone in the colonnades, for huddled some yards away was a very unhappy body language expert. If she wasn't at her flat, maybe she was at his, he'd thought, so got a cab there. No sign. Of couse, he thought, she would be too proud to go there. So he kept the cab, stopping only to pick up his Walkman, and to the bemusement of the driver, made him drive all the way back to her flat. He tried her buzzer again, before suddenly having a brainwave – he'd go to the Heath. He'd walked all the way from her apartment, following the same route as on their second date, hoping, absurdly, to bump into her. He didn't, and ended up at the colonnades. He just sat and waited, hoping beyond reason for her arrival. When she appeared his heart soared, only to come back to earth with a bump with the appearance of Sandip and his champagne. So that was it. She'd brought him and his champagne to their special place.

He just sat there, despondent as hell, as Katie and Sandip sipped their champagne before heading off.

Katie and Sandip wandered back towards the centre of London, as if saying goodbye to the city, and when their legs could carry them no further, Sandip suggested they get a taxi to the museum. Katie had a key, and they wandered in, tipsy, to the vast deserted hall.

Sandip went up to the huge dinosaur skeleton and motioned her over, putting his arm round her. 'Katie, just look at it. Isn't it magnificent?' he said as they stared up.

She turned and looked at him with a giggle, 'Oh no, you're hungry again! You're always hungry! I can't believe it, your stomach is always empty!'

He looked her straight in the eye, and said calmly, 'I'm not hungry.'

'You're not?' She was confused – he was thinking those same words again, *Jee chahta hai ley loon tumhare shebaab kaa russ* . . . so why was he saying he wasn't hungry?

He shook his head, and, with a frivolous air, brought about by champagne and lack of sleep, announced, 'I never was.' She said the phrase again – that's what he'd been thinking, just now and on those other occasions.

Sandip looked her straight in the eye, and began the phrase, '*Jee chahta hai ley loon* . . .' She looked deep into his eyes. He was willing her on by thinking deliberately of the English translation of his words.

'I want,' she said.

'*Tumhare.*'

'To taste.'

'*Shebaab kaa russ,*' he said, slowly, meaningfully.

'Your beauty's . . . juices?' Sandip smiled. She'd got it.

BAM! She walloped him. One hand on each side of the head, instantly felling him. Venomously she snarled at the heap on the floor, 'You little shit!'

Sandip sat up, dazed, but not defeated, 'Of course, I was expecting this. The first attack. The knee-jerk reaction. But where is the second punch?' She turned and walked away from him. He leaned towards her, optimistic that her second reaction would not be negative. 'We are pioneers, Katie. Not just a question of ego. Think of it – our minds fused with our bodies. Get your priorities right.'

Katie was livid. This 'genius', this 'pioneer', was just like every other man. He was the one full of bullshit and his lying words about intellectual passion had led her away from Daniel.

She spun round and kicked him in the stomach, sending him scuttling against the wall and knocking him out cold. 'I just have,' she muttered, before striding out, past a cleaner with one of those trolleys on which every conceivable cleaning utensil can be carried simultaneously.

She walked out into the early morning sunlight, and breathed deeply to try and wake herself up and get rid of the tipsiness and redness in the face. She felt as if something had been lifted from her. She knew she had to see Daniel, and ran across the concourse to find a taxi. There were none as yet, so she hurried along to a rank, and headed off to Daniel's flat. He wasn't there. She buzzed and buzzed and shouted at the window to no avail. She scurried along to Warwick Avenue tube station and dashed home, where she had a shower and some breakfast. She looked at her packed suitcases with an ironic frown. She wasn't going to India. But where had Daniel gone? Not the States, she knew that, so maybe somewhere else on business. She was scared. Had he spent the night with someone. Lucy? He'd told her he'd been upset at the time but glad and that it was definitely finished, and Katie had believed him, but, perhaps after the trauma, and the failure of Harry's visit . . .

Harry! She could ring Harry. Perhaps Daniel was staying with Harry and Caroline? She shuddered when she recalled that dream. It was only a dream, though, and she didn't really doubt Daniel's innocent protestations. Should she call Harry? No. She would go to the Self Centre, and see if Daniel was there, and if not, she'd ask Harry. Wiping some toast crumbs from her scarf she headed out of the door again, and arrived at the Self Centre as the first seminars were getting under way.

In Daniel's seminar room the class were all seated in their leather swivel chairs, listening attentively to Parris. Parris. He and Julie had passed a reckless night, in which all contradictions between his tough new self and weak old self had been resolved, creating a new dialectic whereby, metaphorically speaking, he had his imaginary gun in one hand, and his iron in the other. He had now come to see

Daniel, to thank him, and to offer his own services in helping him resolve his own romantic difficulties. Parris thought that he could also offer himself as an assistant lecturer, a physical reminder not to take the gun thing too far, or at least to help Daniel in rewriting his course.

He stood in front of the class, a quiet confidence exuding from him, in front of the day's 'set'. It was a mock-up of a street, with a parking meter, next to a double yellow line, on which was 'parked' the remnants of a car being worked on by a 'mechanic', a director friend of Bob Narley, and Bob himself, in full traffic warden regalia. It was Daniel's bit of fun, in which he showed how you could overcome even a seemingly impossible situation.

When Daniel wasn't there, Parris immediately realised he wasn't coming. The broken man he'd seen the night before no longer believed in his own theories, and had clearly decided not to continue lecturing any more. 'He told me himself last night,' he explained to the class. 'It's rubbish. all of it.' The class hadn't seen Parris like this before. Even Bob Narley was impressed. He took off his traffic warden's hat and put it under his arm with his *Independent*, with its virgin crossword. Daniel was never this late, so perhaps Parris was right. 'He's not coming back. Go home,' urged Parris.

They all looked at each other for a moment. Parris certainly seemed to know something, and continued strongly, 'Go on. Go,' so much so that the men rose, and, giving each other looks of confirmation, decided to head out. The mechanic followed, and Bob Narley had little choice but to slink out after them.

'Dickhead,' muttered Parris.

Katie came running through the doors. No Daniel.

'Where is he?' she asked nobody in particular. She caught Parris just as he was leaving. 'You! You saw him,

194

where is he?' Parris looked blankly at her. He guessed she was looking for Daniel, that she was the one upon whom Daniel's games had foundered. 'Damn! You don't know!' she cried. She stood, twirling one of the chairs round and round, desperate now. Maybe Daniel had gone away, maybe he'd gone to the States, just to spite her.

Parris asked her, 'You don't know where he is?' She shook her head, and Parris continued, 'Do you know you don't know?'

'Yes,' she snapped. This wasn't helping her, and she twirled manically.

'I'm sorry, then,' said Parris. 'Julie, you see, she just knew.' He felt very sorry for Katie, and for Daniel. He'd said that Daniel's lectures were all rubbish but he didn't really believe it. Although the course had taken him to the brink, something positive had rubbed off. In the same way he could see that Daniel's misfortune in love had given him a much-needed humility. Parris left to go home. Julie and he had a lunchtime rendezvous planned.

Katie dashed along the corridor, looking for the Therapy Room, but Parris's words kept running through her mind ... Did she know she didn't know? What did that mean? That she did know, really? She found the Room but no Harry. Somebody came by, and said he never worked on Thursday mornings. Perhaps he was off with Daniel somewhere. Perhaps they were doing more of that combat game, playing at soldiers somewhere?

Suddenly it struck her. She knew where Daniel was. He had to be there. She ran out of the building, and, checking her purse, saw that she had just enough cash for another cab. She'd spent a lot on cabs recently, but that's what a dinner party wag had once told her. Being in love meant spending more on taxis and eating too much. That was before she hit him.

195

She paid the taxi, and apologised for the smallness of the tip. It was all she had left. And then she ran. Through the woods on Hampstead Heath to their secret section. She'd felt uneasy taking Sandip there. She'd known it wasn't quite right. It belonged to Daniel and her, and nobody else, and that's where she'd find him now. Breathlessly, she called his name as she ran up the stairs to the colonnades. She screamed it louder and louder, and when she reached the top, she knew he'd be there, beaming.

He wasn't. Suddenly she felt exhausted. The night without sleep, the trauma of breaking up, the preparation for India weighed her down. No-one around. Daniel must be with Harry. Or in America. Or with some other girl. It was her own fault. She began to weep. A pathetic sobbing. It was hopeless and she'd been stupid to think he'd be here. Of course, he was getting on with his life. She saw a tear fall from her face to the ground. But she heard something very faint in the distance, a tinny sound.

It was Mozart's *Requiem*. She followed the sound, and quietly said his name. And again. She was getting nearer the source of the sound. Then she saw him. Huddled in a corner, shivering, looking like he hadn't slept, listening to his Walkman with the sound turned right up. She approached him. He turned. He looked up at her. Astonishment, bewilderment, relief surged across his face. He took off the headphones, but stayed huddled as he stared at her with longing.

'You *were* here last night,' said Katie. He looked at the ground, then slowly, uneasily rose to his feet. She stared at him, overjoyed to find him. He padded towards her, until their foreheads touched. She stared into his eyes, and he embraced her. A long, long embrace, as they shivered with cold and delight, anxious to hold each other. He broke it a moment to look at her pupils, then kissed her passionately.

196

She broke away and whispered, 'I love you.' He kissed her again and held her tight as she said, 'I'll be your Mrs.'

As they headed down the steps, clasping each other's hand for joy, she told him she wasn't going to India. She explained that coming here last night with Sandip had made her think only of Daniel, and how Sandip had shown his real intentions. She kept stopping to look at him and say how stupid she'd been, and kiss him. He just grinned, and all he could say was 'I love you.'

They found a café, and gorged themselves on cappuccino and Danish pastries. She told him how she'd looked for him, and described the man in glasses and brown polo neck. 'Parris,' nodded Daniel.

'He seemed to be dismissing your class,' she said. Daniel was amused by this, and thought it only fair. Katie explained that what Parris had said had made her think, and described how she'd looked for Harry and eventually came to the Heath.

'Harry!' blurted Daniel, a piece of raisin from his Danish flying out of his mouth. They had to tell Harry and Caroline that everything was all right. Katie was mortified, but Daniel reassured her that things would be all right again. But they had to do something.

'Where is Harry, though?' asked Katie. Daniel grinned. 'At home, with Caroline.' Ever since Clare had been old enough to go to a child minder, Thursday had been the day she went and Harry made sure he had no clients Thursday mornings. Even though Clare was now at nursery school every day, Thursday retained its special status.

Only today wasn't so special. Caroline and Harry lay in bed, not facing each other. Caroline was still livid that he could have suspected her. Harry was livid that he could have suspected her. He'd compounded matters by agreeing with Daniel that she shouldn't flirt with him. He'd slept very badly. All his most stupid comments, said in the midst of the argument, kept coming back to haunt him. Caroline had slept as badly, and she knew that Harry didn't really think she was having an affair. He'd said sorry enough times, but she didn't feel like accepting his apologies last night. Harry wondered about whispering, 'I love you,' to see if she was awake, and if he was forgiven yet.

Suddenly a car horn sounded. Beep-beep! They both stirred. Beep-beep! They ignored it. Beep-beep-beep-beep-beep! Caroline looked up, and when Harry leapt out of bed she pulled the duvet over her head. Harry opened the curtains. Katie was the beeper, insistently pressing the horn of Joe the Florist's van. Joe smiled at her as he sat in the driver's seat. Katie ran across Harry's front garden, where Harry read, in large letters made of flowers laid on the ground, SORRY BUT WE ARE IN LOV. Daniel was finishing off the V.

Harry stared open-mouthed as he was joined by Caroline. They looked down, bleary-eyed, then at each other, tenderly, and Harry asked, 'Caroline, can you read my mind?'

Without looking at him, she said, 'Right now, yes.'

'Good!' he hissed with childish glee. He looked at her, and pulled her to him, and gave her the big, unequivocal kiss which he'd been wanting to give her all night. They each took a curtain and shut them.

In the garden, Katie was bemoaning the lack of an E to finish off LOVE. Daniel was unfazed. He made her lie down, and with him, they would make the E. This was easier said than done, given that, between them, they had enough limbs to make the letter but not while they were still attached to their bodies. They did their best, each in a sort of foetal position, their legs being the top and bottom bit, and their arms being the middle bit.

After a short while like this, Daniel murmured, 'Have they seen us yet?'

'I think so.'

'You're not sure?' he observed. 'Hallelujah,' he yelled, 'she's human!'

She slapped him, and asked, 'How long do we have to stay like this?'

'Why?'

'Why?' she squealed. 'Because it's embarrassing!'

'No it's not.'

She looked at him with teasing admonishment, 'You're a sex maniac. You're a control freak.'

'Anything else?'

'Yes. You're doing an awful impression of the bottom half of the letter E.'

He looked at his legs, 'Oh.' She was right. 'OK,' and he turned over to try and be more E-like. 'How about this?'

'Awful.'

'OK, how about this. Bend your knees,' he tried to make their knees become the middle bit. It was ridiculous.

'Ridiculous,' she said. So he leaned over and spread her legs, and did the same himself. This was not good. Now they were like two Ys. 'No,' she exclaimed.

Daniel took a breath and said, 'What about this?' before climbing on top of her, pressing his lips to hers. She didn't resist.